A
Modern
Love Story

KATHY WINSLOWER

DEDICATION

To the countless dreamers who find solace and inspiration in the pages of this book, may its words ignite your imagination, stir your emotions, and accompany you on your own extraordinary journeys.

CONTENTS

CHAPTER ONE

MADELINE SCOTT

I collect my things from the cafeteria table, hiking my tote bag higher on my shoulder. My best friend, Emma, is talking, but I barely hear her. My focus is on the schedule for today's classes that I hold in my hand.

"What do you say, Maddy?" I snap out of my thoughts and glance at Emma, who's looking at me expectantly.

"Come again?" I feel bad for asking her to repeat herself, but I wasn't paying attention. I have been stressed for the past few days due to the upcoming show that the drama club is going to put on, and the professors have not been lenient with assignments and projects.

"I asked if you were down to come to the party at Lenny's this weekend." Emma grins, not at all fazed by my distant attitude.

"I don't think I will be able to make it." I shake my head, tucking the braided strand of hair that fell on my face, behind my ear. "I want to practice after hours. The play is supposed to be perfect, and it doesn't help that we chose Shakespeare." I add and watch as my best friend's face falls.

"That sucks. I heard that Lenny is going to throw an absolute banger. Never mind, we can go next time." She shrugs as she drapes an arm over my shoulder.

"Just because I won't be able to make it doesn't mean that you shouldn't go either." I give her a sideways glance.

"I'm not going without you. In the three years we have known each other, have I ever gone to a party without you?" Emma raises a blonde eyebrow at me, and I shrug. Well, that's true. We never go anywhere without each other.

"But you should. I don't want you to miss having a good time because of me. Moreover, I think Lenny would be happy to see you." I wiggle my eyebrows at her. Emma's cheeks turn red as she looks away from me.

"No, I don't think that would be the case." She mumbles, but the blush on her cheeks and the hesitance in her voice tell a different story.

"Come on, admit it, woman. You like him," I say as we walk out of the cafeteria. It's just the beginning of the day, but I needed an iced coffee desperately, and I was late, so the campus cafeteria coffee it was. It isn't the best coffee out there, but it does the job.

"I don't." Emma elbows me slightly, and my grin only widens.

"You have a separate folder for your pictures with him in your gallery. Quit lying," I point out, and she squeals, slapping a hand over my mouth.

"Too loud. You're talking too loudly, Maddy," she hisses in my ear, making me chuckle against her palm.

"You're so paranoid, Em. Lenny isn't going to hear me—" I begin as I remove her hand from my mouth when someone cuts me off.

"What am I not going to hear?" A male voice asks, and I pause, glancing at my best friend, who has paled several shades. Her blue eyes bounce to the person behind me, and a flush creeps up her neck.

"Lenny," she chokes out, her voice strained. I give her a dry look as I watch her open and close her mouth like a fish. And she didn't want me to be obvious? For God's sake.

"Hey, Lenny," I turn around to look at the man of my friend's dreams. He stands there in a blue t-shirt and washed jeans, looking at her expectantly. There is a spark in his brown eyes which tells me he is as happy to see my friend, just as she is to see him.

"Hello, Maddy. Hello, Em," he addresses the two of us, running a hand through his brown hair. I grin at him as I elbow Emma subtly, indicating her to get a grip on herself.

"How are you doing?" I ask, trying to engage him in conversation, partly to let Emma compose herself and partly to steer him away from what he heard.

"I'm doing great. But I do want to know what it is that you guys didn't want me to hear," he replies, and my smile turns wobbly. Of course, he is not going to let it go. Asshole.

"I don't know what you're talking about. I was just asking Em if she was going to your party this weekend. Heard it's going to be a banger," I grin at him, trying to be as real as possible. I know the art of deceiving people.

I'm an actor after all, but when it comes to my friends in real life, acting becomes a task even for me. But there is an alternative to lying. It involves me keeping my mouth shut, but well, that is a little bit too difficult for me to do.

"I hope both of you will come. It would make me quite happy," Lenny pats his chest right where his heart is, and I see my friend blush once again from the corner of my eye. If she keeps acting like a lovesick idiot, the second idiot in front of me will notice what is going on with her.

"I won't be able to make it, but Em will go," I chirp and feel Emma pinch my back. She is standing close enough to me that Lenny doesn't notice. I rein in a yelp as I keep smiling at the man in front of me. She's going to pay for this later.

"That's great!" Lenny turns to Emma, who shakes her head vigorously.

"Actually, I need to finish a few assignments this weekend. I won't be able to make it," she says, and I mentally facepalm myself. I don't know what is wrong with this woman. Lenny likes her, and she likes Lenny, but she goes to extremes to make him believe that she is not interested in him.

"Oh, that's too bad." Lenny rubs the back of his neck, disappointment scrawled across his face. "Try to make it, though. It would be good to have you there." He smiles at Emma before walking away.

I whirl to face my best friend as soon as he's out of earshot, with a scowl on my face. "Are you fucking kidding me? He totally wanted you to be there." I hiss at Emma, who looks like a tomato. I know I shouldn't be so harsh with her, especially when she just had a ten-minute interaction with her crush, but I can't help it.

"I don't want him to think that I'm desperate. Moreover, you aren't going to the party," she points out, her expression the epitome of innocence. I feel the urge to bang my head against a wall because this is insane.

"Emma, baby," I inhale deeply as I say. "You need to make Lenny see that you are interested in him. I mean, don't throw yourself at him, but don't avoid him every chance you get either. It is not helping either of you." I smile at her.

"If you're so good at showing interest in your crush, why don't I see Steven Jones around you?" Emma asks, using the only defense she has left. Steven Jones. It is a low blow, but it works.

"Steven doesn't like me. But Lenny on the other hand, does like you," I respond, scowling at her. I don't like to be reminded of Steven Jones often.

And there are plenty of reasons for it, my top

two being:

1-He is the captain of the soccer team and so very far, out of my league, and

2-He is friends with people who make fun of people like me.

"You never talk to Steven for him to decide if he likes you or not," Emma replies. I turn around and begin to walk, not wanting to engage in this conversation anymore.

"I think we both know why I don't talk to him. The jocks are like vultures. They will devour me immediately after Steven kills me with a rejection. Moreover, after what happened with Jason, I don't think I'm ready to step into the dating market," I say when I feel my friend falling into step with me.

"Jason was an asshole, please. Moreover, isn't there a possibility that Steven might not actually reject you?" She points out. While she has a valid point, I still don't feel safe approaching Steven. He's called Steve around the campus. Everyone knows him, and almost half the female population wants him. The other half has already slept with him, so I am not too eager to fall into line with them, when I know I have a huge chance to be tossed aside because I belong to the drama club.

It is even worse that I'm the captain of the drama club at UCLA. It's like I'm the biggest nerd people know, even though I like to think that I'm pretty cool.

"How have we strayed so far off the topic?" I narrow my eyes at Emma, feeling discomfort churn in my gut. I'm not one to let the comments and names others call me affect me, but I'm human. I don't like to think about my imperfections or rather qualities that people have collectively decided belong to losers.

"You deserved it, for what you did in front of Lenny," she sticks out her tongue at me, and I roll my eyes. I'm not mad at her. She is right though. I deserved it, and I know she would never make me do something that I don't want to do.

"Alright, I won't force you to go to Lenny's party. Let's drop the subject?" I raise my eyebrows, my voice pleading.

Emma grins and nods her head. "You got it."

"You're such an ass," I chuckle as we make our way into the building. Emma and I part ways as I start walking down the hall toward my first class of the day. I enter the class to find that it is full already. Everyone has taken their seats, and I make my way to the one at the back of the class.

Even though, I am not afraid to be myself, I still do my best to not engage or attract unnecessary attention to myself. I don't feel like letting other people make fun of me, just because I gave them a chance to. I call it self-preservation.

I dig out my notebook and pen from my bag and put it on the table in front of me. The professor has not yet arrived, so I take the time to write down a schedule for the theater students so that everyone knows when and where to show up for practice. We have a group on Instagram, so that I can post the schedule on it for everyone's convenience.

As I jot down the schedule, it occurs to me that I will have to leave some time for myself. I needed to go apartment hunting today, and if I make a strict, jam-packed schedule, I won't be able to.

I have been apartment hunting for the past few days, but none of them have turned out to be a yes for me.

Although, I still don't know what exactly I'm looking for, honestly. Since I have been living in the dorm and didn't think that I would ever need to look for another place to live until the end of the year. But then I got a job at the cafe in town, and it is quite far from campus. I can take public transportation, but that would require money too. It's just inadequate usage of my hard-earned money.

Since I have a tight budget, finding a fancy apartment is out of the question, but I do wish to find one that doesn't look like it has been occupied by rats of all shapes and sizes for the past few centuries. I shudder at the thought as I write the schedule again. I feel someone plop down in the seat next to mine but don't look up. It is not until I do glance up at the professor's voice that I see who is occupying the seat next to mine.

Steven Jones glances at me, offering me a small smile, and my heart drops to my stomach. Am I dreaming? Is this a joke? Or did he really just smile at me?

***

CHAPTER TWO

Steven Jones

Madeline looks at me with wide eyes as if

I have grown a second head. I don't know what to make of her reaction. I mean, we weren't the best of friends. Fine, we aren't even acquaintances to say the least, but I'm pretty sure it is rude to stare at anybody like how Madeline is staring at me.

"Are you okay?" I ask her, my voice low. She seems to snap out of her trance at my words and nods her head, looking away from me. "I'm Steve." I introduce myself to her. In the three years I have been studying in the same university as her, I have never introduced myself to her. Today was a different day though. I needed to talk to her.

"Yea, I know who you are," she responds, her gaze flickering over to mine for a moment before returning to the notebook in front of her.

"You're Madeline, right?" I too knew who she was. I have known her for the past three years, but it is only now that I seem to have found the courage to approach her for the first time ever. Her green eyes look hesitant as she glances at me again.

"Maddy," she whispers as the professor begins teaching at the front of the class. "My name is Maddy."

I knew that, too, but it would have been weird

to use her nickname when this is the first time that I have approached her. And moreover, I don't want her to think that I am a creep who knows everything about her because I've been obsessed with her for the past few years, ever since I saw her performing on stage during the orientation ceremony our freshman year.

"Hello, Maddy." I speak slowly, keeping one eye on the professor. I don't want him to think I'm not paying attention in class even though technically, I am not. I don't usually talk to others or am distracted during a class, but then again, never before has my seat partner been the girl I have had a crush on for three years now. "I need to talk to you. Can you wait for me after class?" I ask her.

I feel her body tense next to mine, and I can't help but wonder if I said something wrong. I don't usually make girls uncomfortable. Usually, they are the ones who make me uncomfortable, but it doesn't matter because Maddy looks ready to burst out of her skin.

"Why?" She asks after what seems like ages. The small braids that she always puts in her hair fall into her face, and she tucks them behind her ear. I find the gesture oddly mesmerizing, or perhaps, this is my first time talking to her, being so close to her, and it's messing with my brain.

"It's important. I promise you that I won't waste your time. Trust me." I assure her. I have a reputation around the campus when it comes to girls, and well, others in general. Being a jock is not easy. It comes with a negative reputation and people assuming that I'm an ass to everyone that I meet. I don't like it, the reputation, the negativity that surrounds it, none of it.

"Alright." She nods her head, her lips pursed.

Her eyes are full of doubt, and this time, I am the one who looks away. I can't bear to see the way she looks at me as if she is afraid of what my motives are, as if this is one big prank I'm playing on her.

I slowly inch away from her a little to give her as much space as I can and let her know that I'm not trying to invade her space or lure her in for a prank. I dig my phone out of my pocket and click open Instagram, half-listening to the lecture as I pull up Maddy's profile.

I click on her stories and scroll through them to the first one. It is a picture of an empty apartment with the caption that she's searching for an apartment. This is the reason why I want to talk to her. I want to know if she has found a place to stay. I saw the story yesterday and even discreetly asked around about it.

It turns out that Madeline is looking for an

apartment near Café Rosa, which was a cafe in town where she had recently gotten a job as a barista. She wants to find a place to live, which is near the cafe so that she doesn't have to commute from campus to the cafe and vice versa every day. I have never been so happy for another person's problem before because I have the perfect solution for her.

I don't live in the dorms. My father bought me a house a few miles away from the campus so that I can focus on my studies and not engage in whatever it is that goes on in the dorms. My parents' words, not mine. My parents thought that they were doing me a favor by buying me the house, but it got really lonely there in the past three years.

But, it is the last year of university, and I don't want my mental health to get any worse than it already is. I know better than to ask my parents if

I can get a dorm room, so I have been looking for a roommate, and Madeline can be that for me. Café Rosa is close to my house, so she can walk there every morning if she wants to, or I can drop her off. I wouldn't mind doing that in the least.

Moreover, it is the only way to get to know her. My friends aren't fans of the people in the drama club, and Madeline is the captain. I don't want them to know that I relate to her in any way, but still I want to get to know her. I want to see if there is a chance that we can be together. My friends don't really care about my personal life, so I'll be fine letting Madeline stay at my house for the year. That is my plan, and I hope it works out in my favor because otherwise, I will be graduating with a weight on my chest.

***

As soon as the lecture comes to an end, I shift closer to Madeline, who's packing up. I play with the cap of my pen as I watch the students leave. Once I make sure that every one of them has left the class, I turn to Madeline, who's eyeing me already.

"So, what do you want?" She asks, and her voice is less nervous than it had been when I talked to her at the beginning of the lecture. It makes me nervous if I'm being honest.

"Did you find a place?" I ask in response to her question. Her expression falls before her green eyes narrow into thin slits. A suspicious expression takes over her face, and she leans forward.

"How do you know that I'm looking for a place?" She hisses, her voice dangerous, and so is her expression and stance. I lean away from her, offering her a wobbly smile to calm her down.

"I saw your Instagram story. You said that you

were apartment hunting and then posted a two-paragraph rant about how you hate that there are no good apartments in LA," I point out and watch as she blinks at me, pulling away.

Her cheeks turn a deep shade of red as she tucks one of her braids behind her ear. I feel like it's a nervous tic of hers, but I don't mind it. It's kind of cute. I feel my subconscious rolling its eyes at me. Of course, I would find it cute. Everything about Madeline is cute, more than cute even.

"Yeah, I did put up quite a few angry rants on my stories. Why do you ask, though?" She looks at me, slightly tilting her head to the side. The suspicion is gone from her voice, and I'm glad for it. Because it definitely was not helping my situation.

"I was wondering if you would consider moving in with me at my house." I hide one of my hands under the table as I dig my nails into my palm. The pain drowns the roaring in my head. I don't know what I would do if she said no.

Madeline's eyes widen, and she searches my face as if looking for signs of deceit. I feel my cheeks heat up because even though I do get girls left and right, the distrust in their eyes when I first approach them is palpable. Some of them purely go home with me for a hook up, only because I am Steven Jones, the captain of the soccer team.

"I'm sorry, what?" She balks at me after a beat of silence, as if she had lost her voice for the past couple of minutes.

"I was wondering if you would consider—" I begin to repeat myself for her sake, but she shakes her head.

"I got it. I meant to ask you why on earth

would you let me move into your house?" She asks, and I am certain I look like a weirdo. But years of acting like a jock comes in handy, and I school my expression into one of cool indifference.

"You are looking for a place to live, and I'm looking for a roommate. I thought why not ask you if you would be willing for a arrangement like that," I explain to her, trying not to wince.

"What about the rent?" She questions, and I find slight comfort in the fact that she hasn't dismissed the idea altogether.

"No rent," I quickly say. "The house is mine, and my parents pay the bills, so I don't need you to pay rent. That is why I thought I'd ask you. It is a win-win situation for both of us," I add.

"Why do you want a roommate, though?

You've been living alone for the past few years, haven't you?" Madeline asks, cocking one red eyebrow at me. I find more satisfaction than I'd like to admit in the fact that she knows this much about me.

"Yes," I sigh. I decide to be real with her for a moment because there is no way I will be able to convince her to move in by being dishonest. "I'm tired of living alone. It's a big house for one person, and it gets lonely there sometimes. I am hoping that having company around will help me cope with the boredom." I glance at my hand under the table and the fist that I have clenched.

"Oh." It is all Madeline says. I don't dare to look at her in case the extent of my vulnerability is displayed on my face. I'm not used to talking about my feelings with others. It feels weird. My parents have never been interested in knowing how I'm doing, and neither have my friends. I am pretty sure the only reason I have as many friends as I do is because of my title as the team's captain and because my parents are famous names in the country.

"So what do you say?" I ask once I have gathered myself. I peel my gaze away from my hand and glance at Madeline. She's chewing on her bottom lip, and I find my eyes glued to the movement. My cheeks heat as I realize that I'm staring. I clear my throat, looking her in the eye.

"I will have to think about it," she smiles as she gets up, picking up her tote bag. "I will let you know when I have decided. Just give me a little time." I nod my head in understanding, even though my heart falls to my stomach. Flashing me a beautiful smile, she walks out of the classroom, leaving me alone with my thoughts.

***

CHAPTER THREE

MADELINE SCOTT

"He did what?!" Emma squeals, slamming her hand on the mattress. "Oh my God, Maddy. That's such good news!" She adds, making me frown.

"What is good about this situation?" I ask her. We are in my dorm room, and I have just finished telling her what happened with Steven after class. He had introduced himself as Steve.

"What is not good about this situation? Your secret crush of three years just asked you to move in with him into his house," Emma points out. When she says it like that, it does sound tempting, but then there are other things that I can't ignore.

"Em, what if this is a prank?" I ask Emma, putting my hands on her arms to stop her from jumping anymore from excitement. "What if he's just messing around with me?"

My best friend frowns, searching my face. "Why would he do that?"

"I don't know," I sigh. "But I do know that drama club students, especially me, are not favorites among Steven and his friends. What if this is one elaborate plan to embarrass me?" I shudder at the thought. I don't want to assume the worst of people, but when a guy who has not once, talked to you in all the three years you have been studying together, starts showing an interest all of a sudden, being cautious is obviously the wise thing to do.

"Why don't you ask him if he's serious about you moving into the house?" Emma suggests.

"And make it look like I'm scared of him and his little pack of friends?" I raise an eyebrow. I don't like jocks. They are self-centered assholes. I don't know why I'm so attracted to Steven and have been pining over him for so long because usually, one won't see me in a fifty-mile radius of his kind.

"So you're going to turn him down?" I shrug at Emma's question. I don't know what I will do. I don't plan to give him an answer right away. I will have to think about it, especially when such a large part thinks that he is playing a trick on me. I don't want to be that stupid nerd who falls for a jock's pranks, not ever.

"I don't know, Em. I start at the cafe tomorrow, and I still have a few apartments to check out this evening after practice. Who knows? Maybe I will find one that I like." I smile. I don't feel as confident as I'm trying to be, and that's fine. You don't always feel your strongest. Sometimes, being unsure is okay. Being uncomfortable is okay.

Emma nods, but I can see the words on her face. She wants to say more but she doesn't, perhaps gauging my mood. I don't think I want to hear any reasoning at the moment. Self-preservation over reason any day for me.

***

The apartment is as shoddy as every other I have seen in the past week. The toilet seat is in the worst possible condition, and I feel as if it will break the moment I place my butt on it. The real estate agent shows me around, but even he looks like he doesn't want me to choose it.

"This is the bedroom?" His words come out as a question as he gestures around the four-by-four room that he refers to as a bedroom. I scan the place. A small mattress is pressed against one side of the wall. There is not much room for anything else except for an armoire that is pressed against one wall. "It comes fully-furnished." The guide flashes me a smile that makes me shoot him a look that says, 'Really, buddy? We're doing this?'

"There is barely any place to furnish," I respond, shaking my head and backing out of the room. "This is not what I'm looking for in a place. This is not livable." I make a face, looking around the place.

"Ms. Scott, with the budget you have given me, this is the best that you will find in the market," the man responds, making me wince slightly. Alright, he didn't have to be so harsh about it.

"I am aware that my budget is not too much, but I was counting on you to find me a good deal at a place which is at least suitable for human beings to live in." My tone is sharper than I intend it to be as I narrow my eyes on the guide.

"This is the only place where I can get you a good deal. The rent is well past your budget, but I can talk to the landlord—" I cut him off before he can get another word out.

"What are you guys charging so much for? This place is barely hanging by a thread. You want me to pay a ridiculous amount of money for a room with rats, snakes, and whatnot?" I question. He has got to be kidding me. This place seems to be overflowing with pests if the condition of the mattress and toilet is any indication.

"I'm just the mediator, Miss. I don't set the prices. However, I can negotiate with the seller, but I can't give you anything more than this," he says, ignoring my question. I inhale deeply, trying not to let the hopelessness set in just yet. This was the last apartment of the evening and it has proved to be a waste of my time too.

"It's fine. I find someone else, who can give me what I want." I try to threaten him, but the real estate agent doesn't budge, looking at me with a stoic expression. I sigh and walk out of the apartment. I decide to manage for the next few days until I can find another way. Who knows? Maybe the commute from campus to the cafe wouldn't be so bad.

***

"Goddammit," I mutter under my breath as I put on the apron in the back room of Cafe Rosa. Sweat drips down my temples, trickling down the side of my face and disappearing into my white shirt. The commute from campus to the cafe has been awful. This is the third day at my new job, and I can already feel myself growing tired of it, or rather, the fact that I have to ride here on a bus full of people who don't know basic human etiquette.

"You okay, Maddy?" Riya, my co-worker, asks as she pokes her head into the changing room. I grunt in response, hanging my bag on the hook by the door. "Rough morning, huh?" She asks, her expression softening.

"Some people seem to have missed the lessons on manners we get in kindergarten," I grumble as I tie my red hair up into a bun and walk toward the door.

"Believe me, darling. I have to stop myself from teaching a lesson or two to some most days," Riya jokes, and I crack a smile because I feel the same. She pats me on the back as I walk out of the room and follow her to the front counter.

In the past three days, I have successfully failed to find a decent place where I can live. The real estate agent has stopped answering my calls, and I have a feeling it has something to do with my rude behavior toward him the other day. The stress of finding an apartment along with my hectic schedule has started to get on my nerves, and I can feel myself inching toward my breaking point.

The cafe is pretty quiet at this time of the morning, but the rush hour is close, so Riya and I get to work, putting fresh pastries on display in the front and making coffee. I pull out all the ingredients that we might need today, humming under my breath to dispel the annoyance I feel.

As I grind fresh coffee beans, I feel myself slowly relaxing. Other than acting, coffee is the only thing that brings me a peace that most people would envy. I decide to make myself an iced coffee before the first customer walks in, so I can be nice to them at least, after the morning that I have had.

Our manager, Lisa, who is also the owner of the cafe, has given us full freedom to enjoy coffee whenever we want it. The only condition is that there shouldn't be any customers around. It is one of the perks that comes with working as a barista and also the reason, why I applied for the job in the first place. I make myself a nice iced caramel coffee, groaning as I take sips of the delicious drink.

Riya chuckles from where she is cleaning the counter, her eyes sparkling as she says, "You really like coffee, don't you?"

"Why do you think I took this job?" I ask, taking another sip of the sweet goodness as I move on to fetch some ice from the freezer in the back.

"Fair enough," I hear her reply as I disappear into the walk-in freezer. Riya is a nice woman, and we have become fast friends in the few days that I have been working at Café Rosa. She is from India, but with a bubbly personality similar to mine, and also a lover of theater. She works part-time as a barista and in her evenings, provides private tutoring to students in multiple languages.

Since the moment I met her, I was impressed by her, and the more time that I spend with her, the more I like her. She has an infectious smile, and I feel drawn to her. She is just like me in a different font, and I think I'm pretty enjoyable to be around.

The bell above the front door of the cafe chimes as I walk out of the walk-in freezer. "Maddy, can you take that?" I hear Riya's voice coming from the back room and hurry my steps as

I confirm back to her.

Dumping the ice in the cooler, I walk up to the front counter. But when I see who the first customer of the day is, I pause. Steven Jones looks back at me from across the counter, with a small smile on his lips.

"Good morning, Maddy," he says, his deep voice seeming to reverberate through my body. Or is it just the fact that this is the man I've had a crush on for the past three years.

"Good morning," I respond when I realize I'm just staring at him blankly. "What can I get for you today?" I ask, pasting a smile on my lips. It's not hard. I am used to smiling at people because my mother used to tell me that you never know when your smile brings a sense of joy in to someone's life. But since Steven and I had a questionable and very confusing conversation the other day, I can't help but feel as if my smile is forced.

"I'll have a blueberry muffin, please," he answers, pointing at the tray of muffins in the display. I raise my eyebrows, unable to keep the surprise off my face. Steven doesn't come off as a man who would like something as sweet and delicious as a blueberry muffin. I thought that douchebags only drank beer and had soggy cereal for breakfast.

"Coming right up," I murmur as I reach for the muffin and place it in a brown paper bag. "Anything else?" I ask as I put the packaged goods on the counter for him to pick up.

"Actually, I wanted to ask you if you gave my proposal any thought." His words make me freeze. I glance at him, his blue eyes boring into mine as I try to come up with a suitable response. I wasn't expecting him to bring it up here, but I guess he just did.

"I don't know, Steven," I begin, but he cuts me off.

"Steve. Call me Steve, please." Something in his voice makes me obey him. I nod my head as I swallow.

"Steve, although I think your offer is quite generous, I don't know if I want to take you up on it. Why do you want me to move in anyway?" I ask, frowning. I think if I had a solid reason, I would be able to make a better decision. It is not every day that a guy asks me to move into his house, you know.

***

CHAPTER FOUR

Steven Jones

"I told you, I need a roommate and you need a place to live. It's the perfect arrangement," I said, raising an eyebrow at Madeline as I explained. I didn't know why she was so reluctant to take me up on my offer. It was beneficial for her. She wouldn't have to pay rent or any of the bills.

"Yes, and that is what's making me skeptical,"

she replied, narrowing her eyes at me. I knew this was probably an inappropriate time to notice it, but she looked incredibly sexy with that expression on her face. "Why would you ask me to move in when you don't get anything in return?"

"I am getting something out of it," I pointed out, running a hand through my hair in frustration. Another café employee walked out from the back area, at that moment, and I turned pleading eyes on Madeline. "I am getting your company if you decide to move in with me."

"Is this a prank, Steve? Because I swear to God—" Madeline began, but the woman who had just walked out interrupted her.

"Be nice to the customer, Maddy," she scolded her gently. I watched as Madeline's eyebrows knit together, and she shot me a look of displeasure.

"Can you please cover for me, Riya? I need to talk to this customer," Madeline said. I didn't really like the tone of her voice because it didn't seem promising in the least, but I decided to let her have this conversation with me.

"Go ahead." Riya seemed confused but didn't stop Madeline as she walked out from behind the counter. Grabbing my arm, she pulled me into the back of the cafe where no customer who would walk in would see us.

I was too distracted by her hand wrapped around my arm to pay attention to the murderous glare she had settled on me.

"I just don't believe that you are simply kind enough to just offer me a place in your house, only because you want my company," she snapped. "I have been thinking about your offer for the past three days, and the more I think about it, the more bizarre and suspicious it seems to me."

"I don't know how to make you believe me, Maddy, but I only want some company around the house," I sighed, my shoulders sagging. "Do you know how it feels to live in a two-story house all by yourself? It gets fucking lonely," I added, leaning against the wall beside me.

Madeline searched my face, her mesmerizing green eyes that were lined in black eye-liner, were still full of suspicion. The fact that she didn't trust me stung a little, but I couldn't blame her. If a random guy asked me to move in with him, I would be skeptical too.

"Maddy, what can I do to win your trust?" I asked when she didn't say anything. She seemed to snap out of her trance at that and pursed her lips.

"Why don't you ask one of your friends to

come live with you?" I raise an eyebrow, ignoring my question altogether.

"Because they don't want to. They like it in the dorms," I answer truthfully. I haven't asked them to move in with me outright, but I have hinted at it before, and none of them agreed or took me up on it.

"Alright..." She draws the word out, a hand coming up to play with her silver nose ring. She looks away from me, her gaze fixing on a point over my shoulder. "Bring me coffee every day after school, and then we'll talk," she adds, making me frown.

"What?" I ask, and she settles a flat look on me.

"You asked me how you could win my trust. Bring me coffee every day after classes and before

I go to drama practice. I am not going to move in with a random classmate. I need to get to know you a little at least," she answers. Relief floods through my chest, and I feel the urge to hug Madeline.

"You got it, roomie!" I grin, and she rolls her eyes.

"Don't get too excited. I still haven't decided if I want to move in for sure," she says.

"You will, Maddy. You will." I wink at her as I back away from her. I embody the personality of the jock that I have been for the past few years.

"Don't be too confident, captain. You might be disappointed," she answers, but I walk away, waving at her over my shoulder. I will make her trust me. I can't possibly let go of this chance of having a roommate, someone I can share my life with, someone who will make me feel less...alone.

***

My father stares at me from the other side of the screen, his face set into the stoic expression he always wears. My mother sits beside him with a magazine in her hand. She pretends to be reading, but I know she is listening to every word that passes between my father and me.

"How's soccer?" My father asks, taking a puff from the cigar in his hand. I hate that thing. I hate the smell of it and what it does to the human body. But I know better than to reprimand my father.

"It's going well. We have a game next week. Coach is positive that we will win," I answer, hoping my response would satisfy my father. It obviously doesn't.

"It's foolish to be overconfident right before

the game. You never know what will happen. Overconfidence gets in the way of discipline and focus. You should know that, Steven," he says, and I feel myself lowering my head as I nod.

I sit in the living room of my house, the house that the man on the screen bought for me because he didn't trust me to be disciplined and focused on my goal, by living in the dorms. Even though I'm alone, his words send shame and embarrassment, coursing through my chest. I feel small. Insignificant. I feel like a disappointment.

"I'm sorry, Dad," I apologize. I don't know what I'm asking his forgiveness for, but I know it is the right thing to say.

My father nods, taking another drag from his cigar. He blows out the smoke as he continues. "What about your grades? You didn't email me your grades for this semester."

I feel my cheeks heat at his words. "I forgot. I will send it immediately," I reply, scratching the side of my neck.

This conversation keeps getting worse, and I feel a heaviness descend upon me.

"You should be more mindful, baby," my mother speaks finally, closing her magazine and putting it on the table in front of her. "Are you eating? Did you check out the meal plan I sent you last week?" She asks, and I bite the inside of my cheek.

"Yes, Mom. It was delicious," I force a smile on my face as I lie. I haven't bothered to try any of the recipes on the meal plan because none of them seemed appealing to me.

"Which one did you try?" Her face lights up, and I curse myself. I think back to the meal plan and search for a name I can give her.

"I don't remember the name of the dish, but it was a salad with sprouts, chicken, and avocados…" I trail off as I stare at my mother, hoping she would buy it. She seems to think about it, and my heart thunders in my chest. I feel a time bomb ticking in my head as I wait for her to respond.

"Ahh, yes! I tried that out too. It was too much for me but delicious nevertheless," she responds finally, and I sigh inwardly. That was a close one. I smile as I nod my head when my father's phone rings. He glances at it, and his expression hardens.

"I have to take this, Steven," he turns to my mother, and a silent conversation passes between them.

Even through the screen, I feel left out. I feel

as if I am not a part of their life anymore.

"We will talk to you later, honey. Take care. And keep me updated about the recipes you try." My mother is the one who reaches forward to end the call. I say my goodbye as the line goes dead. I sigh in relief and fatigue as I lean back against the couch. I don't know if it is possible for someone to get tired of their parents, but I sure am.

I unfold myself from the couch and walk out of the living room and into the kitchen. I'm feeling hungry. But then I remember that I need to catch up on all the assignments that I missed in the past week because of soccer practice. Since we lost the last game, the coach was furious. So he made us practice extra hours, telling us to catch up on the assignments over the weekend.

Speaking of the weekend, I need to ask my friends what the plan was so that I can set up a schedule according to it. I still need to maintain a reputation and keep up appearances as well as juggle university and soccer.

It is not easy, I will admit, but I have become used to it now.

I dig my phone out of my back pocket and dial Logan, one of my teammates and the man who always has all the news about everyone around campus. When you ask him how he knows so much, he just says that he has his sources. I have a feeling that the sources he refers to are the girls, whom he hooks up with on a daily basis.

"Yes, Captain?" Logan's voice sounds through the speaker, and I straighten.

"What's the plan for the weekend, my man?" I ask, sounding like the person I hate the most. Sounding like a douchebag jock who has nothing better to do than smoke pot and sleep around the campus, every chance he gets.

"Lenny is throwing a party this Saturday. We're all going there. And on Sunday, I was thinking about getting some practice done in the morning, before getting wasted in the evening. What do you say?" He asks. For the ass he is, Logan is the only one who cares about soccer as much as I do. The other friends in our group don't really care about the sport but rather the reputation that comes with being on the team.

"Sweet. I will meet you guys there, then." I begin to pull the phone from my ear when I hear Logan speak.

"Hey Steve, a few of us are heading over to the diner in town tonight, for some dinner. You down?" He asks, and I think about it. I need to get done with the assignments, but I'm afraid to say no. I know for a fact that Logan will ask me the reason for canceling the plan with them. And I also know how uncool and 'unjock-like' it is to be studying in the evening instead of going out and having fun.

"Yeah, I will be able to come for a couple of hours. I still need to wake up early tomorrow for practice." I lie. I decide to make an appearance and then slip out. Then, I can study the whole night. It's not a big deal. I have done it before.

"Great. I will let the others know." Logan hangs up, and I pocket my phone. I glance around the kitchen and shrug. I guess I don't need to cook tonight.

***

CHAPTER FIVE

Madeline Scott

I stumble into my dorm room at seven in the evening, every part of my body exhausted from the past few hours of practice. My roommate, Ellie, looks up at me from her laptop as I walk to my bed, dumping my tote bag on it.

"Emma came by looking for you. She just left a few minutes ago," she tells me, and I nod, trying to catch my breath. These damn stairs kill me every time, reminding me how infrequently I exercise. The elevator has been broken, since forever.

"I will call her. Thanks for telling me," I smile at Ellie, panting. She eyes me for a moment before tossing me the water bottle from her nightstand.

"You need to start running around the track, Scott. You look like you've been trampled by a bison," Ellie makes her observation, to which I wince. Well, ouch.

"I just need to get used to these damn stairs," I respond once I have chugged half the bottle of water. I massage my aching foot with one hand as I sigh, "It might take me some time, but I will get there."

Ellie shrugs, closing her laptop and turning to me. "How is practice?" She asks, and I purse my lips as I think about it.

"We're getting there. 'Midsummer Night's Dream' is a fun play to enact, but it's Shakespeare, so it's tricky. And I want it to be perfect," I answer, getting comfortable on my bed.

"I saw your Instagram story earlier. I think you guys are doing really well," she points out, and I grin.

"Thanks! I hope we are. I am excited for this one," I tell her. The tickets will be available for purchase from next week, and I am hoping for the show to be sold out.

"Good luck," she gives me a smile, which I accept gladly. Talking to Ellie, who make me feel motivated to go after what I want, fills me up with energy. I am about to tell her that, when my phone rings.

I answer it, bringing the device to my ear. Ellie

turns her attention back to her laptop, and I turn to the call. "Come to my room. Now. It's an emergency," Emma says, and before I can say anything, the line goes dead.

I pull the phone away from my ear and blink at it, wondering what the hell just happened. "What happened?" Ellie asks, and I shrug.

"It was Em. She wants me to come to her room. Says it's an emergency," I reply as I get up from my bed. Climbing down two floors is the last thing I want to do, but I know better than to not show up to Emma's room when she's asked me to.

"You better go," Ellie chuckles, and I nod, smiling. I pocket my phone, willing my legs to stop hurting and slowly walk out of the room.

I make my way to Emma's floor and knock on

the door, hoping she opens it right away. The door to her room flies open almost immediately, and she grabs my arm, pulling me inside.

"Whoa. Calm down. What is going on?" I ask, looking around the messy room. Her roommate, Gianna, shakes her head from where she stands in the middle of the disaster.

"She got a phone call, and then she went haywire on her clothes," Gianna says when Emma doesn't respond. She just drags me in front of her cupboard, which looks very bare, and turns to me with her eyes wide.

"Lenny asked me out," she turns a deep shade of pink. "He caught up with me after class and asked if I wanted to go on a date with him," she squeaks out the last part.

I feel a grin tug on my lips.

"I told you!" I squeal as I launch myself at her. Engulfing her in a hug, I mumble, "I'm so happy for you."

"Thank you, but now I need your help." She pulls away from me and points at her clothes, which are all over the room. "He called me to tell me that I should wear something fancy for our date tomorrow, and I don't own anything fancy," she adds, her lips turning down in a frown.

"That is it?" Gianna balks, and I suppress a cackle. "You went bonkers because you don't have a dress. Jeez, woman, you could have asked me," she scolds Emma, who looks sheepish.

"You are unbelievable, Em," I shake my head, and she pinches me on the arm. I yelp as I take a step away from her. My ankle gets caught in a pair of jeans lying on the floor, and before I can regain my balance, I fall on the floor with a thud.

My butt lands on a cushion thankfully, but my head hits the wall behind me, and I grunt in pain. I hear Emma break into a fit of laughter as Gianna rushes to my side.

"Oh my God, are you okay?" She asks as she offers me her hand. I shoot Emma a dirty look as I take her hand, rubbing the back of my head. My vision goes blurry for a moment, perhaps from the impact of the fall as I narrow my eyes on my best friend. "Asshole."

"You deserved it," she giggles as she walks up to me. "Does it hurt too much?" She asks, stroking a hand down my hair. I smack it away as I lean into Gianna, allowing her to pull me back to my feet.

"Traitor," I mumble as I walk to her bed, carefully this time.

"I'm sorry," Emma says between her giggles as

she walks up to me and settles beside me. "I freaked out." Her laughter dies down slowly, and her gaze drops to her hands, which are clasped together in her lap. "I didn't expect Lenny to make a move," she shrugs.

Gianna took a seat across from us on her bed and snorted, gaining our attention. "You're probably the only one who didn't expect him to make a move. Lenny has been looking at you with heart eyes since the start of the semester. Everyone noticed it except for you," she pointed out, and I nodded my head, agreeing with her.

"The man doesn't let go of any chance to be around you. It was about time he grew a pair and asked you out," I shrugged. Emma's cheeks turned red as she blushed. She's the sweetest girl ever, and I leaned forward, wrapping an arm around her.

"Don't worry about the dress, Em. You can

have mine. I brought a few for a party my parents wanted me to attend. You can borrow one," Gianna said, her voice reassuring. Emma's shoulders relaxed under my arm, and she shot her a smile.

"Thanks. I should have asked you before going 'Hulk-mode' on my wardrobe." She glanced at the mess she made, and I chuckled.

"I will help you with the cleanup," I assured her, and she leaned into me. Gianna glanced at the time on her phone and cursed, getting up from the bed.

"I will see you guys later. I need to meet up with Jared. He and the guys are going to the diner in town for dinner," she said as she walked over to her cupboard and pulled out her purse. Slinging it over her shoulder, she shot us a smile before walking out of the room.

"I still don't believe that she managed to tie Jared down," Emma mumbled as the door closed behind Gianna. I agreed with her. Jared used to be a known playboy at the university, but once Gianna caught his interest, he didn't look at any other girl anymore. It's been a year and a half since they started dating, and he has given up on his playboy tendencies of sleeping around.

"He is probably the only one from the group who can be tied down," I said after a moment.

"Steven could be open to being tied down. If you ever decide to move in with him, that is," Emma shot me a knowing look, and I rolled my eyes.

"Not again, Em," I replied, but then the interaction from this morning came back to me. "He showed up at Cafe Rosa today," I added, looking away from my best friend.

The squeal I was expecting from her pierced my ears, and she scooted closer to me.

"What did he say?" She asked, her face lit up with excitement.

"He was trying to convince me to agree to moving in with him," I told her and watched as her eyes widened. A smile stretched her lips.

"What did you say?" Her voice came out all squeaky, and I raised an eyebrow at her, asking, 'Really?'

"I told him that I didn't trust him enough to move in with him and he had to earn my trust," I shrugged.

"What did he say then?" She took my hand in hers and squeezed. I frowned at her excitement and wondered if the situation with Lenny had gone to her head.

"He agreed," I answered. "Why are you so excited about this?" I added, searching her face. She looked delighted.

"I am so happy for you. Your one-sided love story is going to turn two-sided finally," she responded, placing a peck on the back of my hand.

"Honey, he just wants a roommate, not a girlfriend," I smiled as I pulled my hand from her grip. I loved Emma, but she could be delusional at times, and I mean the crazy kind of delusional.

"We'll see," she patted me on the cheek. "We'll see." I did not like the look in her eyes one bit.

***

I walk out of my last class for the day, ready to

be done with practice and go to my room and crash. I can take a nap for fourteen years straight. But I don't need a nap at this point; I need to fully hibernate. I haven't been able to get any sleep with practices after classes that go on late in the evening.

Then, the next morning, I have a job to show up to, before classes start. I have been barely getting any rest with such a tight schedule.

I make my way down the hallway, turning left when all the students turn right to walk out of the building to get back home. I hike the straps of my bag higher on my shoulder as I hurry down the quiet hallway. As I am about to enter the theater room, a hushed voice calls out my name.

My heart jerks in my chest from the sudden sound in the otherwise silent hallway, and I glance over my shoulder, looking for the source of the voice.

A head peeks from behind a classroom door, and I frown as I try to get a better look.

"Maddy. Here." A hand beckons at me, the gesture urgent. I walk towards the hand, even though I probably shouldn't. I doubt it is safe to listen to a voice in a deserted hallway when you don't know who it belongs to.

I walk over to the voice anyway and sigh when I see it is Steven. "What now?" I ask, my voice nothing more than a hiss. The hallway is all too quiet, and I'm pretty sure if I speak loudly, it will echo through the corridor.

"Jeez. Someone woke up on the wrong side of the bed," he answers, smirking at me. I feel the urge to slap the look right off his face, partly because it reminds me that he is a jock and partly because he looks ridiculously good with it.

"Really, Jones?" I raise my eyebrows. "I doubt at this rate, you will be able to convince me to move in with you." I know it is a low blow, but it works. Steven's smirk drops, and he offers me a genuine smile. It looks even better than the smirk. Dammit, Maddy. Get a grip.

"I'm sorry. I just wanted to give you this," he says, extending his hand forward. It is then that I notice the cup of coffee in his hand. I grin as I take it from him, sipping from the straw. I nod, impressed that he nailed my order to the 'T'.

"Good job!" I pat him on the arm. "Keep it up, Jones, and I'm all yours." The moment the words leave my mouth, I realize what I just said. I glance at him to find him looking at me with an amused expression on his face. My cheeks heat as I shake my head. "I mean you will get me to agree to your offer if you keep this up," I stammer.

"You're cute." He pats me on the cheek, and I feel myself turning red. "And I'm confident that I will get you to take me up on my offer." He winks at me as he steps out of the room and begins to walk down the hall. "See you tomorrow, Scott." And with that, he turns and disappears down the hall.

***

CHAPTER SIX

STEVEN JONES

I pant as I plop down on the grass in a quiet corner on the field, uncorking the cap of my water bottle and taking a deep drink. The sun beats down on my head, and I lean against the wall behind me. We are fully done with practice today, and I can finally go home and get started on my assignments. My professors have been kind enough to extend my deadline, but I still need to do more work in the little time that I have.

Logan walks up to me as I put the cap back on the water bottle and place it beside me. "Care to share, Jones?" He asks, gesturing at the bottle.

"Help yourself." I toss him the bottle, which he catches effortlessly. Taking a seat beside me, he drinks his fill as I scan our surroundings. Logan is probably the closest friend I have. We don't talk heart-to-heart or sit together and share our problems, but I still feel more appreciated and myself in his presence than with any of our other friends.

"What are your plans for tonight?" He asks, panting a little as he puts the bottle between us. I glance at it as I contemplate what to tell him. This is what I hate about being myself in the university. I have to always weigh my words, always make sure it is something a jock would say.

"I have a few assignments to get started on.

Then I'm free. Lenny's party is tomorrow, right?" I ask, and Logan nods.

"How are you dealing with these assignments, man?" He groans, leaning his head back to look up at the sky. "I feel like throwing up every time I think about them."

"I'm powering through." I chuckle. "It's not easy, but do we have a choice?" He grunts in response, picking up the water bottle once again and pouring the rest of the contents on his face and chest.

"I expect you to fill it up for me now." I give him a sideways glance. He flips me off, and I shake my head. What else did I expect?

"Can't your father just pay the teachers or something to give you good grades?" Logan asks a moment later. I turn to face him, expecting him to be joking, but he looks dead serious. Bro has no idea what goes on in my family, what my parents expect of me, so I can't even blame him.

"I don't think so. Even if he could, I doubt my father would." I shrug. I don't expect him to ask me more about it or at least ask me if I need to talk about it or if I'm okay. But even when he doesn't, I can't help but feel a sting of disappointment, rising in my chest. Who am I kidding?

"That sucks." He makes a face before getting to his feet. "Come on, let's get to the locker room before the other guys get the good shower." He gestures for me to get up.

I grin as I do, burying my feelings and misery deep down inside of me where I can't hear them. I follow him toward the building, my gaze straying to the part where I know the drama club meetings are held. I wonder what Maddy is doing, if she has given my offer any thought today. I even gave her the coffee she asked me to bring her, but she didn't tell me if I have won her trust enough to get her to move in with me.

She's cute, I will admit. I mean, I knew that before. There was a reason I had a crush on her, but I didn't know her, back then. She was just Madeline Scott who talked a lot and loved acting, but now that I have talked to her, she's more charming and funny than people give her credit for. And a little crazy, if the way she manhandled me in the cafe was any indication.

I want her to be my roommate, now more than ever, not only because she is my crush and it would give me a chance to get close to her, but because she seems like a genuinely good person. As I make my way into the boys' locker room, the fuzzy feeling in my chest that I get every time I think about Madeline is replaced by a suffocating weight. I need to pretend again.

As I pass by the guys, grinning at some, cracking stupid jokes that I don't find funny in the least bit, but laughing at them regardless, I feel myself disappearing a little more. Steven Jones will vanish soon if I don't get someone to pull me out because I've tried. I've been trying to pull myself out of this pit for the longest time but I can't. And I need someone's help now. I'm humble enough to admit it.

***

The assignments are a pain in the ass. I'm absolutely over with studying and I'm contemplating throwing my laptop and notes out of the window when my doorbell rings. I jolt in my chair, surprised because no one comes over to my house. My friends are not allowed since my parents have strictly told me that I can't throw any parties in this place and other than my friends, I don't really know many people in the city who would want to pay me a visit.

I get out of my chair, frowning as I wonder who the hell it could be. It's late in the evening, and I don't have a date tonight. Not that I go on many dates. By dates, I mean that I haven't asked a girl to come over for a rendezvous. The women I sleep with occasionally, are the only ones who have set foot in this house other than me.

As I make my way down the stairs, all kinds of scenarios go through my head. What if my parents decided to give me a surprise visit? I wouldn't put it past them to show up unannounced at my doorstep because they were worried about me.

I swallow and shake my head, discarding the thought as I walk up to the front door. I unlock the door and pull it open, freezing when I see the person standing on the other side.

"Maddy?" I ask as I take in the woman in front of me, fidgeting as she glances over her shoulder and then back at me.

"Hey. I'm sorry I showed up unannounced, but I thought we could talk?" She says, her words coming out as a question. I blink at her for a moment because I still can't wrap my head around the fact that she's standing in front of me, on the front porch of my house. "Steve?" She asks, waving a hand in front of my face, and I snap out of my stupor.

"Of course, come in," I quickly respond, stepping to the side and opening the door wider for her. She steps inside, walking past me deeper into the foyer. She looks around as I close the door behind me and turn to face her.

"How'd you find my address?" I ask because I don't remember ever telling her where I live.

"I asked my roommate. She's been here apparently," she answers, still looking around the foyer with what I can only put as a surprised expression.

"Who's your roommate?" I ask, frowning. I have brought a lot of girls over but I don't remember all of their names, and I'm not a creep, so I don't know who Madeline rooms with in the dorms.

"Ellie," she replies, and I nod, remembering her. She's a nice girl, especially in bed, but that's not the point. I shake my head, discarding the images and memories. Sometimes, the jock shows up unexpectedly, without me wanting him to.

"Oh right. So, what do you want to talk about?" I ask her as I lead her into the living room. Her gaze once again strays around the room as she enters and takes a seat on the couch, still distracted.

"I…" She trails off as she scans her surroundings. "You have a beautiful house," she finishes, turning to me. I force on a smile. Somehow, her words don't bring me any kind of happiness. I know that the house is beautiful, but it's a prison for me, a prison where I slowly waste away, every day.

"Thank you," I respond because it would be ungrateful of me to not appreciate what I have. I am aware that some people would kill to have the house where I live in as a college student, but I'm over it. It's not mine. And it reminds me every day that my strings are in someone else's hands. My parents are the ones who decide what I do in my life. And this is the most rebellious thing I've ever done, asking someone to room with me. If my parents ever come to find out…

"I am here to talk about your offer." Madeline's voice pulls me out of my thoughts. I'm glad because I was spiraling there for a second. She looks nervous as she glances around once more before saying, "When can I move in?"

Her words send a shock careening through my chest. I am rendered speechless for a moment and have to compose myself before I ask, "You want to move in? Really?"

I know I probably shouldn't sound so excited, so relieved. I'm a jock. I'm supposed to take life one moment at a time, not bothering about the people in my life or the consequences or results of a certain situation, but right now, I can't bring myself to suppress the relief that I feel.

"Yes, I do. I've been thinking about it, and I think it would be better for me," she answers, tucking one of her braided strands behind her ear. She does that so often, but every time she repeats the motion, I find myself tracking it.

"That's great. You can move in anytime you want to," I tone down the enthusiasm in my voice. I need to remember who I am for Madeline. I have to remind myself that the others at the university don't know anything about my personal life and situation.

"Alright, but I want to pay you rent," she looks at me, determination lining every inch of her face. I frown, pursing my lips.

"You don't have to. The house is mine, and it's basically free for me to live in. You don't have to pay me anything," I don't want her to stress over rent. It's one of the reasons I asked her to stay with me so she doesn't have to pay rent, doesn't have to waste her earnings from the job at the cafe.

"I know, Steve. But I can't do that. Moreover, the students at the university will talk if I stay here for free. I don't want that either," she answers, chewing on her lower lip. It is then that I realize that maybe I'm not the only one who struggles with my image, that maybe there are others who feel the same way, who feel the need to change or hide. Maybe it is the way the world is. And the realization that perhaps I'm not alone, makes another wave of relief wash over me.

***

CHAPTER SEVEN

Madeline Scott

Steven is reluctant about me paying rent, but I'm adamant too. I'm known to be the stubborn one, in my family. There is no way that I'm going to back off. I don't want to be a burden for him, and I don't want to come off as a freeloader to his parents when they find out that I'm going to be staying with him.

"Two hundred," I say, crossing my arms over

my chest. For the past fifteen minutes, we've been discussing how much rent I will be paying him. I don't know why on earth he would want to say no to the free money. He frowns and shakes his head.

"One-fifty," he bargains. I make a face. We started from five hundred, and it's come down to one-fifty. I don't know how I feel about losing this bargain.

"One-seventy-five," I argue. He opens his mouth to speak again, but I put a hand up to cut him off. "One-seventy-five is a very affordable rent, for me to live in a mansion like this, okay? We've been going back and forth for the past fifteen minutes, and I have allowed you to lower the rent to a hundred dollars, but no more. I'm going to leave if you don't allow me to pay you this much at least."

An emotion crosses Steven's face, but before

I can put a finger on it, it's gone. I wait for him to respond, hoping he agrees to this arrangement. I am well aware of how he and his friends view people like me. And I will be damned if I allow them to pick another limitation in my character.

"Alright," he sighs finally, and I suppress the grin that threatens to make its way onto my face. Until this morning, I had no plans to agree to his offer, but I think it is the best thing to do. Public transport, I've come to realize, is not the safest form of transportation, and I got to experience that firsthand. That was the final straw for me.

Moreover, for the past week, Steven has been bringing me coffee after classes, and before I'm headed to drama practice. He's always alone and makes sure that we're both alone, where no one else can see us, but I don't particularly care. He said that he would bring me coffee to win my trust and convince me to move in, and he has done it. So here I am.

"So when do you plan to start moving in?" He asks, once we've decided that I will be paying him one hundred seventy-five dollars every month as rent. I'm sure that I will be able to manage the rent. It's affordable, and I'm secretly glad for Steven's reluctance to let me pay.

Why? Because I'm still a student. Even if I know that I need to pay the rent, for the sake of my reputation, I am also happy that I only have to pay so little. This means that I can save more.

"I will try to get my things here by the end of the week. I also need to deal with the university housing board. I will have to tell them that I'm going to move out of the dorms," I reply, and Steven nods in understanding. I have to talk to my parents about it, too. They already know that I'm planning to move out of the dorms, but I have yet to tell them that I have found a place to live, and the house actually belongs to a rich-ass student from my own university.

"Alright. Do you want me to show you your room? Give you a tour of the house?" Steven offers, and I nod eagerly. I would love to have a tour of the house. This place is beautiful, and if the foyer had me questioning my place here, I can't imagine how the rest of the house looks.

He smiles as he gets up from the couch, gesturing to me to follow him. He walks in front of me, and I can't help but notice how tense he looks. His shoulders are slightly hunched as if he's either really stressed or very wary of my presence. I'm not going to hurt him, obviously.

I cannot help but notice the way he looks so out of place in his own home. I love studying people. Another reason why I took the job at the cafe, to have a chance to closely watch, different kinds people, all through my shift. And over the years, I have picked up on ticks and body languages that tell you how a person is feeling. And right now, looking at Steven's back, despite his easygoing attitude and way of talking, I can't help but see that he looks ill at ease.

I want to ask him about it because I'm also a very curious person, but I clamp my mouth shut. We're not in a place where I can ask him intrusive personal questions. We're going to be roommates and nothing more. I don't want to creep him out and then have him decide against giving me a room in his house.

So, I shake off, the way I feel around him, as if his sulking energy sucks out my own. Instead, I simply follow him up the stairs of the house, focusing on the wallpapers and artwork in the hallway rather than his tense shoulders and stiff body language.

***

"A what?!" My father cries, and I wince a little. I'm sitting in my dorm room once again, cross-legged on my bed, and my laptop is open in front of me. My parents stare at me from the other side of the screen, their jaws hanging open. I knew I should have been gentler in telling them that I am going to be moving in with a guy.

"He's a good guy, Dad. I know him." I lie through my teeth because I don't want my father to fly all the way to California to put Steven six feet under the ground. I wouldn't put that possibility, past my overprotective father.

"Sweetie, is it safe, though? Even if you know him, are you certain that it's safe to move into the same house as him? Have you talked to his parents? Has he ever had a roommate before?" My mother asks rapid-fire questions that have me wanting my bed to swallow me whole.

"Mom, I am sure that he will not kill me if I move into the same house as him." I assure her, but my words backfire. My mother's face pales, and she clutches her chest, calling to the heavens.

"Jesus Christ, Madeline—" She begins, but my father intervenes. Thankfully.

"Maddy, baby, do you think you can ask the guy to talk to us? Can we meet him? I will feel much better about the arrangement if I talk to him," he says, and I feel my chest filling with warmth.

Yes, my parents can be too much at times, but the knowledge that they're always here for me, always ready to fight for me, and love me enough to challenge the world on my behalf, brings me relief and security that no one and nothing else can.

"Yes, I will talk to him and let you know. I don't think it will be a problem." I answer, and my father looks visibly relieved. I smile at him to let him know that I know what I was doing. I never make decisions on a whim. I've been thinking about Steven's offer for a week and a half now. He's proven to me that he really does want me to be his roommate, and his reluctance to charge rent money from me also brings me a sort of comfort and confidence in him.

"I still think it is a stupid idea. College guys can't be trusted. I would rather you live in the dorms and we pay the fee, than you moving in with a man," my mother mumbles. I shake my head at her. She's a conservative Christian woman who believes that if a man and a woman are in an enclosed space together, sin follows and whatnot. I haven't really been much of a religious person myself. I humor her sometimes, but I don't really believe in the extreme teachings the church exposes her to, and those which she in turn tries to make me follow.

"Catherine, I think Maddy knows what she's doing." My father puts a hand on my mother's shoulder in a comforting gesture. I am not the only one in my family who doesn't always stand by my mother's beliefs.

"But Harry, how can you let her move in with a man she's not married to?" She asks my father. I roll my eyes as I pull a pillow into my lap and hug it to my chest. I watch silently, as my parents go back and forth with each other. Ellie, who's sitting on her bed, glances over at me, catching my gaze, and offers me a small, awkward smile.

I mentally facepalm myself as I finally intervene in the argument my parents are having.

"Guys, I really need to go now." I lie again. My mother will kill me if she knows that I lied twice in a span of ten minutes. "I will call you later after I talk to Steven. I don't think he will have a problem talking to you guys." I add.

My father nods while my mother just broods beside him, clearly not on board with the plan still. But still, I say my goodbyes and end the call before she can start lecturing me once again about how to be a good Christian woman. I love my mother but I simply don't want to be limited in my potential. I don't want to be told what to do, when to do it, and how to do it. My mother knows this but she tries to change my mind, regardless.

I close my laptop and lean my head back against the headboard of my bed. "So, you're really going to move in with Steven, huh? Lucky girl." Ellie says from her bed, and I nod my head without turning to look at her.

I don't like how she talks about Steven, like he is a piece of meat that everyone should try once and then throw away. It's not just because I have had a crush on him since forever, but also because he is a human being with feelings. And I just know that Ellie, would be quite offended if another man or woman spoke about her the way that she speaks about Steven.

"Don't forget me when you finally do the deed. Because I want all the juicy details." She adds, when I don't respond. I clench my jaw. I am not moving into his house to make him sleep with me. I don't have any interest in sleeping with him. Well, that's not completely true. I like Steven. But sleeping with him is not the only thing I want from him.

I want to have a friendship because I'm pretty sure that we can never be in a relationship and he will look at me the way that I look at him, the way that I want him to.

"Goodnight, Ellie." I sigh as I place my laptop on my nightstand and settle into bed. I pull the covers over my body and close my eyes, willing for the anger to dissipate. I don't want to get into unnecessary arguments when I know that I can never win one. Not with people like Ellie who are popular and liked by the others. Like I said, I have learned self-preservation a long time ago, and I strictly follow the rules that I have set for myself.

***

CHAPTER EIGHT

STEVEN JONES

I stand under the alcove after class, a cup of caramel macchiato in my hand. Leaning against the wall, I scroll through my phone, waiting for Madeline to get out of class and come this way. We had the last class together, but I got out early after finishing my assignment to get to the cafeteria and get her coffee.

The news about Maddy moving into my house

hasn't spread yet, which is a surprise. I have been checking the college gossip page almost every hour for updates. I know for a fact that Madeline's roommate knows about our arrangement, and so does her best friend, so I can't fathom why the news isn't all over the gossip page yet.

I know I should be grateful that we've not been put under a spotlight, but I can't bring myself to relax. The worst happens when you least expect it, so I'm trying to apply reverse psychology here. Maybe if I keep being paranoid, nothing will happen at all. The students won't ask me questions, and Madeline will not be troubled either. Neither of us has it easy when it comes to our social status in the university hierarchy.

"I will see you in three hours. I need to start packing. I will need your help, so don't try to back off at the last moment," I hear Madeline's voice as she appears in front of the alcove, talking to someone, in front of her. She turns around, and her gaze snags on me.

She seems startled, stumbling away a little as she eyes me warily. "What on earth are you hiding in there for?" she asks, and I cringe. I don't think I'm hiding anymore. I think every student on the floor knows that there's someone under the alcove now.

I put a finger to my lips and gesture for her to shut up. It takes her a moment, but then she stops speaking, but not before hissing 'what' twice in a loud whisper. I swear to God this woman has no filter in her mouth whatsoever and is probably lacking some brain cells too.

Reaching forward, I grab Madeline by the arm and pull her sharply toward me before she can exaggerate the scene. "Can you shut up for a moment?" I ask her, my voice barely a whisper.

Her body collides with mine softly as I hide her away from the world with me too.

"You scared me, dickhead. How am I supposed to shut up for a moment after that?" she snaps at me, but her voice has lowered. I thank the heavens for the little mercy.

"I'm sorry. I didn't mean to scare you," I respond, smiling sheepishly.

"What are you doing here anyway?" she asks, and I bring my hand up to show her the coffee.

"Waiting for you so I can give you this." I watch as a grin lights up her face. My heart fills at the sight of the smile. Such a bright smile just for a cup of coffee. I wonder how much gratitude and love toward one's life one needs, to reach this level of happiness, to be happy just to have a cup of coffee.

Madeline takes it from my hand and takes a sip, making a sound of approval. My cheeks heat at the way she simply enjoys her drink. There is something intensely intimate about the gesture. It is then that I also realize how close we are standing and that I have an arm wrapped around her waist. Has she not noticed it yet? I wonder to myself because she doesn't try to step away from me.

But now that I am painfully aware of our proximity. I should have let her go once I had pulled her under the alcove, but in my panic, I had forgotten that I was holding her. Now that I realize it, I feel the heat rush to my face. I want to disappear into a fog. Or perhaps I could pull her closer.

"I need to get to class," Madeline's voice pulls me out of my thoughts. Embarrassment floods with such force that it's a surprise that I'm even standing in front of her until now. I should have been a puddle on the floor. "Anyways, thanks for the coffee, Steve." She grins at me as she takes a step away.

My hand falls from her waist, and I smile at her dumbly as she starts walking away from me, coffee in hand. I want to open my mouth and ask her if she needs help with the moving, but my lips stay glued together.

Madeline stops a few steps away from me, glancing over her shoulder as if she forgot something. "My parents want to talk to you," she informs me. "They want to see the man I will be living with for the foreseeable future. Is that okay?" She asks, her voice turning a tad softer.

I dumbly nod my head again, still caught in the last few minutes and our closeness, the heat of her body, and how it felt under my hands. Oh hell no, Steve. I chide myself as I force myself to nod once more.

"So, do you want to come over to my dorm, or should I come over to yours?" Madeline asks, and to my dismay, it isn't a yes or no question anymore, so I actually have to force myself to speak.

"My place," I find myself saying, my voice breathless. Madeline nods, smiling, unaware of my inner turmoil. Throwing another goodbye over her shoulder, she begins walking again.

I just stare at her retreating figure and wonder, for the first time since I offered her a room in my house, how would I deal with my growing feelings? And most importantly, how would I deal with myself, being in such close proximity to her, all the time? Oh, I'm doomed.

***

I pull at the collar of my shirt, nerves twisting my stomach. I don't know why I feel so anxious. It's just a call with Madeline's parents to convince them that I am not a con man and that their daughter will be safe in my house. But for some reason, my heart is racing, and I can feel sweat dripping down my back. This is ridiculous. I am nervous for no damn reason.

Madeline sits on the couch beside me, leaning forward as she logs into her laptop. She glances at me over her shoulder as the pointer hovers over the FaceTime icon.

"Are you okay?" She asks, her eyes searching my face. I nod, forcing a smile which I'm sure looks as fake as I feel putting it on. Madeline frowns. "It's okay. They don't bite."

"I am okay," I lie again. She purses her lips but doesn't push me. Turning back to her laptop, she clicks on the icon. The call goes through, and I swallow the lump in my throat. I need to put up a good impression because I really need a roommate and I want it to be Madeline.

Madeline straightens herself as a face appears on the screen. I can't make it out because the person is too close to the camera. All I can see is their forehead. I hear Madeline utter a long sigh.

"Dad, you need to move away from the camera," she says. The person moves out of the way of the camera, straightening, and I tense once more at the sight of the man, on the other end of the call. "Hello," Madeline adds, and I glance at her from the corner of my eye to find her grinning.

"Hello, honey," her father responds, his gaze flickering on to me.

"Good evening, sir," I bow my head slightly in

respect because my parents didn't raise a disrespectful brat.

"Good evening," Madeline's father replies, his lips set in a firm, tight line. I feel a drop of sweat trickle down my neck and disappear into my shirt. Oh, this is stressful.

"Dad, this is Steven Jones, the guy I was telling you about," Madeline comes to my rescue, and I heave a sigh of relief. I don't know why, but my voice has left the chat.

"I see," her dad murmurs, his gaze still fixed on me. There is a stern and stoic expression on his face that has me wanting to apologize to him. For what, I have no clue.

"I will be moving into his house," she adds, and I never thought I would get to see Madeline being so awkward, but here we are. I refrain from looking at her with a surprise expression on my face. It's not too hard because I am glued to my spot anyway, and my body feels frozen.

"So, what do you do, Steven?" Her father asks. I clear my throat, willing my words to form on my tongue. This will not work out otherwise.

"I am a student at UCLA with Maddy," I begin, cursing myself for using Madeline's nickname. "I am the captain of the university soccer team and my major is in business studies." I gesture at his daughter with one hand. He nods his head as if turning my response over in his head.

The man isn't dressed half as impressively as my father does, but the air he holds, the aura that I can feel through the screen, is authoritative and intimidating. He sits with his back straight and shoulders wide. His face is grim, and his eyes green—the same as Madeline's—rest on me with a cool indifference in them.

"A business major, huh? What do you plan on doing after that?" He questions, and Madeline gasps beside me. I dare a glance at her this time to find her horrified.

"Dad! What does it have to do with me moving into his house?!" She cries out but not disrespectfully. Her voice is low, and she is still sitting beside me with a poise that only an actor possesses. Her expression looks terrified though.

"I was just trying to get to know the man," her father reasons. Madeline opens her mouth to speak again, but I cut her off. This is my chance. I let the jock speak when I address her this time, letting the confidence seep into my words.

"It's okay. I get that he is concerned about his daughter's well-being. He should be asking me all kinds of questions. It's not easy to let your daughter out into the world, which is not known to be kind," I say, my gaze flickering over to the screen.

Madeline eyes me with surprise and wariness, but her father's expression softens a tad bit. Bingo. The best way to impress a father is to be concerned about his daughter as much as he is and support him in being concerned for her.

"I am hoping to get drafted this season, actually. Business is a subject that I just happen to like and it's a solid backup plan," I answer truthfully. I really want to be a soccer player. There are no ifs and buts when it comes to soccer. That is my end goal. Being a business major allows me to look at the world and the economy with a different perspective, and that is why I enjoy studying it. Plus it doesn't hurt to have a plan B, just in case.

"Ah, I see. So, do you think you are good enough to get drafted?" He asks, and I try not to let his words sting. I don't want to show him that I am insecure in my skill, even though others consider me the best.

"I hope I am. You can come watch my game sometime and tell me if I'm good enough," I offer, letting loose a small smile. Jock. I am glad of the personality sometimes, and this is one of those times.

"I would love to come. Maybe when I come to see Maddy at your house, the two of us can go catch your game, too," he responds, and I feel a weight lifting from my shoulders because even though he didn't say it outright that it is okay for his daughter to stay with me, his offer speaks volumes.

***

CHAPTER NINE

Madeline Scott

I'll be moving in with Steven within the next week. I don't know what he did on the call with my father, but I've never seen my father laugh and joke with a guy, by the end of their first meeting, especially when the guy is somehow related to me. But I'm not complaining because I got what I wanted in the end.

Steven helped me move, letting me use his car

to transport the smaller suitcases while I had to hire movers for the larger boxes. I've been in dorm rooms for the past three years, so quite a lot of stuff accumulated over the years, and only when I had to pack all of them in suitcases and boxes, did I realize how much stuff I've been hoarding.

Even after donating a lot of stuff I didn't need anymore, I had much more than I expected to deal with. But now that the move is done, and I just need to unpack and make myself at home in my new residence.

Steven had been helping me even after I moved in and settled into my room. He takes out at least an hour of his time at the end of the day to help me sort my things out, even though I told him that I can do it on my own.

It makes me want to hug him, but that would be extremely inappropriate, and I don't think that

I should be hugging a guy, whom I've been crushing on for the past few years anyway. Only if I don't want any unwanted consequences, like butterflies in my stomach or my heart thundering as if a storm is going to sweep over my body and mind.

Even though I've been trying my best to avoid making any additions to my current feelings for Steven, my best friend is convinced that we are endgame and are going to end up together by the end of the year.

I think she's bonkers because Steven and I don't talk much in the house, except for when he's helping me unpack.

"I'm telling you, Maddy. This time, next year, I'll be thinking about the names for my future nieces and nephews," Emma wiggles her eyebrows at me, making me spit out the cappuccino that I had been sipping on.

"Nieces and nephews? Lady, you're way too in over your head. Kindly put your thoughts back into your brain," I respond, looking around the cafeteria to make sure none of the other students heard her. I'm not trying to get the rumor mills going. I hate it when people go around spreading false information. It's one of those things that I cannot bear and makes me want to go 'She-Hulk' at everyone who is involved.

"I'm just trying to manifest your dream relationship and love life. Don't be a party pooper," Emma rolls her eyes.

"I'm okay where I currently stand with Steven. We're friends, I guess, and that is good enough for me," I say.

It's partially true. I don't want to complicate

things between us because if we end up together—it's a very unlikely scenario but let's assume—and then we break up for some reason, it will be very hard for me to continue living with him, and I cannot see myself getting a new place in the foreseeable future.

"You are a liar, Maddy," my best friend leaned back in her chair, her untouched sandwich going cold on the plate. "I know you want to date Mr. Captain-Of-The-Soccer-Team-Who-Looks-Like-Henry-Cavill," she added.

"You are dating your dream guy, aren't you? You don't have to worry about me. Live your happily ever after and let me be," I replied.

I wasn't offended by Emma trying to get me to think about Steven being more than just a friend, but I don't like it when people tries to force things on me. At this rate, I would lose all interest in the man once and for all. Maybe Emma's nagging wasn't so bad after all.

"Sweetie, Lenny and I both agree that you need to make a move on Steven, now that you're living together." She patted my forearm, a sad smile on her face. My face fell, and I felt the blood rushing to my ears.

"Lenny? Lenny knows? You told Lenny about Steven?" I asked, stuttering a little as I tried to force the words out.

"No, of course not." Emma looked hurt, and I felt bad for doubting her. But then how did he know about my crush?

"He figured it out on his own, from all the stories that you have been putting up lately about how you're having so much fun with your new roommate," she answered, and I sagged in relief or wariness, even I didn't know.

"So, it wasn't as subtle as I thought it was," I gritted out, sulking in my chair. I traced a finger along the rim of my cup, wondering if Steven had seen my stories and he too assumed that I was talking about him. I hope not.

"It is okay to like him, Maddy. You know that, right?" Em's voice turned gentle, and my heart ached.

"Of course. Why wouldn't it be?" I asked, lying once again. The truth was that I didn't think I was good enough even to think about Steven romantically. I didn't think I was deserving of having a crush on him, much less being in a relationship with him. I knew it was stupid to think the way that I was thinking, but I couldn't help it. I was on the last rung of the social ladder, perhaps even lower, and he was at the very top.

"Maddy, you are not undeserving of Steven." Emma's hand wrapped around mine, and I wondered if I had said my words out loud or if she had just gotten good at reading my expressions.

"I don't want to talk about it," I shook my head, pushing thoughts of a possible relationship and also of the man whom I was roommates with, out of my head.

I willed myself to relax before forcing a grin on my face. "Our practice has been going so well these days. I am so excited for the show!" Hoping that it would change the subject. I didn't like being sad, especially over things that had no place in my life, in the first place.

"I am sure you guys will be great," Emma responded, getting the hint. A smile lit up her face too, and I relaxed in my seat slightly. "I want to come to visit you during practice, but I can't get away these days. I am so sorry," she gave me an apologetic look that I waved off.

"It is okay. I know it can get hectic, especially with the art club," I grimaced as I remembered the first time I had accompanied Emma to the art club. It had also been the last time.

A crumpled ball of paper smacks me in the back of my head, and I freeze. Emma's gaze lands over my shoulder, and from the way her face pales and she appears uncomfortable in her own skin, I already know who threw the ball at me.

Heels click against the cafeteria floor, and I brace myself. I've grown accustomed to this presence and I was familiar with the footsteps of the person whom I know will appear in front of me in a matter of seconds.

I hold my breath as Gia walks into my line of

sight. I don't say anything, waiting for her to speak. I don't usually engage with her and rarely respond to what she has to say to me. It has been a few weeks since she last bothered to bully me, but I guess she has taken an interest in making my life hell once again.

"I see that you're the lead in the upcoming play," she says, placing her hands on the table and leaning forward. I'm keenly aware of every pair of eyes in the room, which has come to a halt on us. I want to tell the students to mind their own business, but I just stare at Gia, waiting for her to continue. "I wonder if the role is that of a harlot." She smirks as if the insult will get under my skin.

"If you had paid attention in seventh grade, Gia, you would know that 'A Midsummer Night's Dream' doesn't have a character who is a harlot." I smile politely at her, earning snickers from the other students. Like I said, I usually don't respond to Gia, but sometimes, when my patience is already running thin, and it snaps, whatever is left of it in half.

Her face falls, and she looks around with a thunderous expression. She turns back to me, her eyes narrowing.

"You've been talking back to me a lot lately. Don't forget that I can get you kicked out of classes with a snap of my fingers," she threatens, snapping her fingers together for emphasis. I shrug as I turn to my coffee, disregarding her, even though her threat does leave a sour taste in my mouth. I know very well that Gia can get me suspended or even expelled if I annoy her enough.

But despite the warning bells ringing in my head, I find myself saying, "Don't you have anything better to do than go around in your six-inch heels, which you don't know how to walk in, by the way, and insult people who are trying to eat in peace?" I raise my eyebrows at her, glancing briefly at her high heels, which I know she'll be carrying in her hand by the end of the day.

"Be very careful about what you say, Ma-de-line. Shortening your name to Maddy doesn't make you a badass or popular. You're just a stupid nerd who's a wannabe actor. Your place is here and will always be here," she points at the floor. I wonder if she really thinks spewing crap like that, which it seems she has picked up from some 2000s movie, is going to break me and have me begging for her forgiveness.

"Gia," someone calls from behind her, and she straightens. The voice is familiar, and when I look up, I find Steven and his friends standing around a table on the opposite end of the room. The man beside Steven is the one who has spoken. I vaguely remember his name being Logan. "Come on. I thought you will be waiting for me when I came by," he whines, pushing out his bottom lip.

I glance at Steven, who is standing beside him with his arms crossed over his chest and an unreadable expression on his face. It's not the cheerful and cocky expression I spot on his face when he's around his friends. I can't quite place it, but I forget about it anyway when I realize he is looking at me too.

My cheeks heat, and I peel my gaze away from him, focusing on the food in front of me. I'm embarrassed that he had to see Gia treating me like crap. This is not the first time that he has seen her mistreating me, but it is the first time since I started talking to him and moved into his house.

I don't look at the group for the rest of the lunch break, although I'm painfully aware of the laughs and giggles coming from their table. I sigh softly as I brush off Gia's words and strike up a fairly useless and uninteresting conversation with Emma.

****

CHAPTER TEN

Steven Jones

I feel like a moron. Yes, that is exactly how

I feel as I glance at Madeline walking around the kitchen. Her back is turned to me, and she hasn't noticed me yet, even though I have been standing in the doorway for the past few minutes. Honestly, I don't know how to approach her. I feel shame and embarrassment curdling in my gut.

I have been wanting to talk to her, ever since

I got back home after football practice. She had been home already since she didn't have practice today, but I haven't been able to go up to her and say what I want to.

Gia's little stunt in the cafeteria and my inability to defend Madeline or stand up to the bully guts me. It pains me. The only reason why I didn't get involved is that I didn't want to be the guy, whom other people target and try to bring down, too.

Gia would have insulted me as much as, if not more than, she insulted Madeline. And it scared me. It made me stay rooted to my spot and not do anything when she called Madeline untalented and a wannabe. She was not. Madeline was neither of those.

I have seen the woman in action, on stage. None of my friends know, but I have. I have seen all of her plays, all of her shows. I had been there in the last row, in the darkest corner, so no one could recognize me, and I have seen her pour her heart out through her craft. She hasn't been the main character ever before, but whatever character she plays, it immediately becomes my favorite.

I am still lost in my thoughts when Madeline turns around, her eyes landing on mine. She seems startled but she recovers quickly, smiling at me as I pretend to have just walked in.

"You're back? Do you want dinner? I was making some for me," she asks as she goes around the kitchen, picking out ingredients from the cabinets and putting them on the counter. She looks so at ease in my house in the past few days that she has been here, and I can't help but be surprised.

I don't think I have ever been so comfortable

in this place as her.

"It's okay. I can fix myself something. You don't have to trouble yourself," I wave her off, not quite meeting her eyes as I walk to the kitchen island and lean against it, scanning the kitchen as if thinking about what I am going to cook for myself tonight.

"I'm making more than enough for myself. You can have it. Otherwise, it will go to waste," Madeline responds, smiling at me. She looks carefree despite Gia's words from this afternoon. Does she still think about it? Is she trying to hide the pain? I want to ask her, but that would be prying.

"Alright, if you insist," I give in, shoulders sagging.

I make a mental note to cook dinner for the

both of us some other time ,to pay her back.

"Good, because I make the best pasta out here," her grin widens as she turns back to the stove and puts the pot on the flame.

"Seriously?" I cock an eyebrow at her, walking over to her and leaning a hip against the counter. "Now, I will have to try it," I add.

It is good to have someone in the house who is not me or the maid who comes twice a week to deep clean the house. I feel more relaxed than I have in a very long time, perhaps for the first time ever.

"My mother used to make pasta a lot because I love it so much. So, I picked up her recipe. She puts in all these spices, and it's just so flavorful, simply finger-licking good," Madeline tells me as she goes about making dinner. I stand there and watch her talk about her family.

I can't help but notice how fondly she talks of her parents, as though they are her whole world, as though they are her safe place. And maybe they are. Not every parent is like mine. Not every parent treats their child as if they are a means to become famous or well-known or a pet project that would bring them personal validation.

"She used to tell me, 'Madeline, if you don't eat your food, I won't eat mine either.' And it worked every time," she says as she stirs the sauce in the pan, the smell of garlic and seasoning filling the air. I don't remember the last time the kitchen was full of the smell of food, so fragrant. "She would sit me down at the dining table and feed me until every last morsel was in my tummy. And then she would tell me that God was happy with me. I didn't believe it, of course, but I was happy that she was smiling."

She pauses, and I find her looking at the pot with a small smile on her face. I don't know what to say, but she saves me from the trouble of coming up with an answer. "I didn't mean to rant so much. I am so sorry. You must be tired. And hungry. This will only take a minute." She walks away from me before I can tell her that it is okay, that I like listening to her talk.

I am not jealous of Madeline like I expected myself to be, but I am in awe of her life, of her parents who love her so dearly, and of how happy she sounds when she speaks of them.

"You seem really close with your parents," I comment, crossing my arms over my chest. She glances at me and nods, her expression softening.

"They were my first best friends. And I owe them a lot," she responds. Her words don't seem to carry the same weight to her as they do to me.

For her, it's normal to have loving parents. It's quite the opposite for me.

"What about you? Your parents seem to love you a lot from the looks of it," she gestures around the kitchen.

I feel my heart clench, my jaw clenching slightly. A wave of anger washes over me, and I want to ask her if, for her, love is equal to money. I doubt it is because she isn't the richest person out there. Still, her words sting, and it takes me a moment to gather myself before I can speak.

"Yes, they love me." My voice is devoid of any emotions, almost clipped. I tried to sound indifferent, but it didn't come out the way I wanted it to.

Madeline looks at me for a moment, her gaze searching my face. The smile that she had been sporting slips from her expression. I can almost see the questions in her eyes, and before she can ask me anything, I gesture at the stove.

"Is the sauce supposed to be simmering for so long?" I ask. My distraction works because her gaze snaps to the stove, and she curses softly under her breath.

"Shit." She turns the stove off, using the spoon to stir the sauce. I sigh with relief inwardly, wondering, what the hell am I doing here? I don't want to talk about my life and my parents with Madeline. I like her, yes, but I don't want her in the deepest, darkest parts of my life. I don't want her anywhere near the rotten center, because I don't want her running the other way when she finally realizes that I am not the jock I pretend to be, that I am not as whole as I act.

Madeline plates our food while I am still lost in my thoughts. I blink as she turns away, gesturing for me to follow her. I walk out of the kitchen after her and into the dining room where we sit down across from each other.

"Let me know what you think. I want your honest review." She grins at me, pointing at the plate of pasta in front of me. She seems to have forgotten about my little slip-up in the kitchen, and I am beyond grateful for the little mercy. I don't think I will be able to answer any of her questions, even if I want to.

I nod my head, schooling my features into a smile, as I twirl the pasta around my fork and bring it to my mouth. I take a big bite because I am ravenous after practice today. The flavors that burst on my tongue the moment I put the pasta in my mouth have me moaning. And I don't even care because it is so freaking good.

My eyes widen, and I watch as Madeline's

smile widens until it threatens to split her face in half. She looks delighted by my reaction, and I feel a surge of butterflies. I chew and swallow the food, and without a word, shove another forkful in my mouth.

Madeline lets out a laugh then, the sound filling up the dining room, filling up the house. I could swear that the colors brighten at the sound, that the place smiles back at her, at the sound she has granted it. A carefree, beautiful laugh.

"I didn't expect you to like it so much," she says, eyeing my plate, which is almost halfway empty. I shrug, grunting my response. I want to tell her how amazing the pasta is, but I can't stop eating long enough to let her know that. I think it is enough to answer anyway.

Madeline shakes her head, chuckling as she turns to her own food, eating slowly. She closes her eyes as she takes the first bite, licking her lips once she has chewed and swallowed. I can't help but track the movement with my eyes, my throat bobbing.

My senses seem to be on overload because I don't know why else my skin is tingling, and my heart seems to sing. I glance at my plate, not wanting to be a weirdo staring at Madeline. I am pretty sure that she will gouge my eyes out of their sockets if I don't remove my gaze from her face. I don't want her to get the wrong idea. I mean she won't be getting the wrong idea, but I really don't want her to think of me as a creep.

I finish my food in silence because I can't bring myself to stop eating. Once I have scraped every last morsel off the plate, I look up at Madeline to find her already staring.

"Are you okay?" she asks, making me frown.

"Yes, why?" I raise my eyebrows in confusion. I bring my hand up to touch my face, wondering if there is something on my face.

"You looked…" She shakes her head, trailing off. "Never mind," she mutters, changing the subject with the next question. "How did you like the pasta?"

"It was amazing. You shouldn't have made it for me because I am tempted to ask you to forget the rent and cook me pasta every night," I reply, grinning. It is the truth. I would gladly take the pasta over money any day.

Madeline's cheeks turn red as she hides her face behind the stray strands of hair that have fallen into her face.

"Do you always keep your hair up in a bun?" I ask her because I am curious. I don't remember seeing her with her hair down, even during her plays. She always keeps it pulled away from her face. I don't mention that, of course, because that would make me a creep once again, and I am trying to avoid being one. Although, I am already testing my boundaries, a lot right now.

***

CHAPTER ELEVEN

Madeline Scott

I tuck a strand of my hair behind my ear, suddenly nervous under Steven's searching gaze. I'm not going to lie; his question has caught me off guard. I don't know how I'm supposed to respond. I think over his words once more before deciding to be cool about it. No need to read too much into simple questions, that are asked out of curiosity, right?

"I hate it when my hair tickles my neck. And leaving it open, guarantees that it gets stuck to my skin when I sweat," I answer, shrugging a little to act indifferent. I feel the urge to ask him if he notices me so much that he knows I never put my hair down, but of course, that would be a very stupid question. That would have me screaming into the pillow at night, once I realize how foolish it was.

"That's valid," Steven responds, his gaze flicking to my bun as if he can see it from where he sits. I doubt he does. "I'm actually glad I don't have long hair." He adds, running his hand through his hair.

I track the movement with my eyes, my core clenching at the sight of his biceps flexing and his hair falling back on his forehead once he lets go.

"Your hair looks good on you," I blurt out before I can stop myself. I didn't mean to say it out loud, but sometimes, the words just spill from my lips on their own accord and I can do nothing about it.

"Thank you," Steven offers me a smile, but it does little to soothe the way my heart is racing in my chest from saying too much, saying things that I didn't want to say in the first place.

"You—You're welcome," I stammer as I get up from my chair. Enough. I need to get away before I keep blurting things out. I reach for his plate, but he waves me off.

"I can take care of it. Don't worry," he pushes my hand away and stands up. He pries my plate out of my hand too and steps toward the door to the dining room. I let him go, not putting up a fight because honestly, I am quite tired, and I am glad he offered to do the dishes.

I walk out of the dining room, heading to my room to hit the sack because every part of my body hurts and the pasta has me wanting to collapse and go into a food coma. I can hear the sink running as I pass by the kitchen, but I don't dare to peek in. I know I should probably wish Steven good night and let him know that I am heading to bed; I usually do, whenever he is on the same floor or in the same room as me. But tonight, I want to put some distance between us, create boundaries.

Sometimes I get carried away. I like to talk to people around me. I like to take care of the people around me. It is my love language, but sometimes, I say more than I intend to. Sometimes, I do more than what is considered appropriate.

It's not because I am naive but because I like to shower the people I care about with affection and love.

I should mention that, I am absolutely not in love with Steven Jones in any way, but he helped me in a time of need, and I am eager to prove to him how grateful I am for his help. I know I am paying him rent, but it's too little for what he has done for me. But I also need to remember that I am trying to shake off my feelings for him and not trying to make them grow.

In the past three years, it has been easy to disregard these feelings because we weren't around each other. The class we share, which is literature, didn't allow us to be close friends or such. And I liked it that way because then I knew there were actual boundaries between us, a social barrier between us. But in this house, the boundaries are blurred. There isn't a hierarchy that I need to be wary of. Steven is just Steven, not the soccer god. And I am just Madeline, not the drama freak and wannabe actor.

I plop down on my bed after locking the door, pulling the book on my nightstand into my lap and opening to the page that I was reading. I decide to lose myself in fiction because what is a better way to escape from real life?

No matter how happy you are, sometimes you need an escape from reality, from life. I lie down on my bed, holding the book over me as I continue reading. The silence in my room slowly brings back the self-control that I seemed to have been losing control of. I decide to keep a little distance from Steven in the upcoming days, just to give myself time to clear my head and calm down a little.

I turn the pages of the book, my eyes scanning the pages as I get ready for the climax. I have classes tomorrow but only one class in the afternoon, so I am not too stressed about sleeping late. I do have to get to the cafe in the morning though, but I doubt that it would hurt me, if I spend some time reading. After all, I doubt that I will be able to sleep tonight until I am completely spent. I don't want to lay in bed thinking about dinner over and over again or the fact that I loved the way Steven complimented my cooking, indirectly admitted to noticing me, and then went on to look at me with a burning curiosity that no one has ever looked at me with.

***

The rush hour has me running from the counter to the back room and back to the counter like I am a machine and I have wheels fitted into the soles of my shoes. My breathing is heavy, and I almost faint as I ask the next customer what she would like to have. The one other girl, who has been hired to help with the morning rush, has taken the day off, and I didn't think I would ever miss a person as much as I miss her.

"I will take this one. Take a seat," Riya, my coworker whispers in my ear, gently pushing me out of the way. I turn to tell her that it's fine, that I can take this order, but she settles a stern look on me. I sigh as I walk away, putting a hand to my chest to calm my racing heart. No, it's thundering. Thundering as if there can be a storm in my chest at any time now.

I settle down on a stool, out of sight of the customers, and catch my breath. I don't know why I have been feeling so out of breath lately. I want to blame it on me not being athletic, but I don't think an unathletic person would feel like their lungs are trying to collapse in on themselves.

I get up to get a water bottle from the refrigerator and sit back down on the stool, chugging half of it in one go. I feel my breathing returning to normal, albeit slowly. I glance over my shoulder, leaning to catch a sight of what is going on in the front, only to find Riya speed walking through the place, getting the customer what they want. I feel bad for abandoning her, but then I remind myself that she asked me to get some rest.

Once I feel better, I get up on wobbly legs and walk back out. Riya glances at me, a question in her eyes, and I nod my head, giving her a weak smile. I think I should start doing breathing exercises because my lungs seem to be forgetting how to function properly.

I join Riya at the counter again and luckily, I don't feel my breath growing heavy or my chest congested for the rest of my shift. Once our shifts are over, Riya and I get into the changing room to head back home after handing over the duties to the next shift of employees.

"Today was crazy. But the tips were good," Riya says, shaking her wallet at me, her eyes sparkling. I nod my head as I look at mine, filled with all the tips that the customers gave us.

"The customers were really generous today," I reply, pulling my apron over my head and hanging it on the wall beside the door of the back room.

"True. Or maybe they wanted to reward you for working with such poor respiratory health," Riya points out, and I grimace. Okay, ouch.

"I don't know what is up with me. I don't usually look like a cow, panting after walking around for a few minutes," I defend myself. It is true. I have never felt so out of breath before.

"I think you overexerted yourself," Riya comments as we walk out of the back room together. I shrug, digging my hands into the pocket of my uniform and squinting at the sun that seems to be glaring down at us.

"I think I am growing old," I joke, and Riya chuckles, shaking her head.

"You're too young to be that old," she compliments, and I feel my cheeks turning hot.

"Old people can be cute, too," I answer. Riya hums in agreement before she responds. "They are. Old people are probably the cutest amongst us all."

"My mama is scared to be old. I will have to ask you to meet her sometime. You must tell her that old people can be cute," I say, glancing sideways at my co-worker, who turns to look at me with a grin on her face.

"I would love to! Your mama has to realize the beauty of getting old, the relief in the fact that we don't have to live here forever, nor do we have to carry the burden of being beautiful all our life,"

Riya replies. I cock my eyebrow at her statement.

"Beauty is not a burden," I give her an amused smile. I don't think beauty is a burden, and it doesn't really matter the way us humans say it does. I am aware that I belong to the group of people who are said to be beautiful, and I don't think I will ever regret not being beautiful, but at the same time, it doesn't stop me from being bullied, from being picked on.

"Beauty can be a burden for some," Riya looks at me, and I frown, trying to make sense of what she is trying to say. "It can be a boon for many but a curse for some. The only reason why people don't admit to beauty being a burden is because they don't want to assume themselves to be beautiful or embarrass themselves in front of others," she adds.

Her words do make sense now. I can see what

she is trying to say although the concept is still a little vague to me. "Then why do we want to be beautiful, if it is such a burden?" I ask, genuinely curious. I like talking to Riya. Her insights on life and her way of perceiving things are different from most people, and naturally, I want to know more, I want to get her to talk more to me about it.

"Because if we are not beautiful, society says that we don't hold value. But the same society condemns you, envies you if you are too beautiful and meets its standard to a certain limit," she smiles, and I try not to balk at her because that is too real and it hits too close to home.

***

CHAPTER TWELVE

STEVEN JONES

"Another party?" I groaned as I place my head down on my desk, wanting to be anywhere but here in the moment. I didn't know how the students at my university managed to attend so many parties, go to so many bangers, and not even get tired. I was positive that I would pass out even if I just stepped foot into a house with loud-ass music.

I looked around my room, missing the quiet and solace already. I wanted to be alone tonight. I had been planning to curl up in bed and watch a nice movie, maybe ask Madeline to join me. I didn't want to go to a damn party.

I straightened, putting my books away as I tried to coax myself to go. I didn't have a choice, I reminded myself. I needed to keep up appearances, and if I didn't show up with my friend group, then the person throwing the party would be picked at. They would be bullied by people like Gia, and I didn't want that. I didn't want others to feel like trash when I could prevent it from happening albeit indirectly.

I pushed away from my desk and walked over to my closet to pull out the clothes that I planned on wearing tonight. I picked out a simple black shirt and a pair of jeans, dumping them on the bed before going into the bathroom to take a shower.

I didn't want to sound like a self-centered ass, but I was aware that I held a certain power over the students of my university. They looked at me with hope and expectations that I felt obliged to meet. No matter how hard I tried, I couldn't bring myself to disregard the responsibilities that they unwillingly placed on me.

When I first started university, I was okay with being the captain of the soccer team and the popularity that came with it. I was okay with hiding behind the mask that I had to put on around my friends. I was also okay with putting my real self behind because I thought that maybe over the years, I could actually change myself.

Stepping into the shower, I let the water soak me. I let the sound, drown out the world outside and every last bit of sensation. I liked this moment, whenever I was alone or rather when I got to be alone. I place my hands on the wall in front of me, breathing deeply. My eyes were closed, and I let the water beat down around me, washing away every bit of restlessness and anxiety that I felt.

When I stepped out of the shower a few minutes later, I felt better than I did going in. I walked out into my room and put on my clothes. Drying my hair and applying deodorant, I walked out of the room with my car keys and my phone.

I walked down the stairs just in time to see Madeline walking out of the front door. I followed her out of the house, catching up with her on the porch.

"You're headed somewhere?" I asked as my gaze trailed from the top of her head to the tip of her toes. She was dressed in a pair of baggy low-rise pants and a black cropped shirt. Her hair was in a bun once again, and she was wearing heavy black eyeliner and dark brown lipstick. My gaze lingered on her lips before I forced myself to look her in the eye.

It is then that I realize that she has already spoken, and I was so distracted by the way she is dressed and how stunning she looks that I missed what she said.

"Sorry, what did you say?" I ask, rubbing the back of my neck nervously. Idiot. I let a sheepish smile break free, and Madeline searches my face with an unreadable expression on her face.

"I said that I am headed to the party at Chloe's," she replies, jabbing a thumb over her shoulder. Surprise flares in my chest at her words.

"You go to parties, too?" I can't help but ask. I thought that she didn't like social gatherings like parties. I mean not to be someone who believes in stereotypes, but my friends had me convinced that since Madeline is a drama nerd and that parties aren't really her scene.

"What is that supposed to mean?" She asks, crossing her arms over her chest. Her eyes narrow, but all I can focus on is the way her collarbones peek out from her skin, from the movement. I mentally slap myself for being such a jerk. Get it together, Jones.

"Nothing. I just didn't take you as someone who enjoys going to parties," I tell her. I don't want to come off as a jerk to her who thinks of her the same way the others do, because in reality, I don't. She is the most beautiful woman that I've ever met and the most talented, too, and I hope she knows that.

"Well, I do," she responds, sharper than she has ever spoken to me before. Turning around, she begins to walk down the steps of my house. I realize that I have probably pissed her off really bad, so I run after her. Damn it, Steven. Way to talk to a girl you like.

"Maddy, wait." I grab her arm before I can think it through. Pulling her toward me, I turn pleading eyes on her. "I am so sorry. I didn't mean to offend you-" I begin to explain myself. Not very jock-like of me, but I don't care at the moment.

"It's fine, Steve. I am aware of my reputation among your kind. I just thought you were a little different from the others. I sure hoped so!" She snaps, trying to get me to let go of her arm. I hold on, scared that she might run off if I do.

"I am not like them. I don't like to assume things about people, and I don't like to bully others. I have never seen you at one of the parties before, and that is why I thought that you might not like to go to such gatherings." I explain myself completely this time, and she doesn't interrupt me.

Her gaze roams over my face, and I pour every ounce of honesty I own into my expression. I am not someone who likes to make other people feel like shit about themselves. I don't just go on assuming things about people , especially those who I don't know personally, and even if I did, I prefer to ask them about their likes and dislikes. This moment was just a slip of the tongue for me.

"You did sound like them, right now," Madeline comments, but she has calmed down. Her chest rises and falls with heavy, quick breaths, but she doesn't seem ready to rip my neck off.

"I'm sorry, I messed up. I meant to ask you if you liked parties and went often. That totally came out wrong," I confess, giving her a small smile, hoping she accepts my apology. She purses her lips, a frown settling between her brows as if she is thinking. A moment later, she nods.

"Alright. I forgive you." She yanks her arm out of my grip this time. I let her go. "But if you assume something about me the next time and sound like an ass while doing so, I will kick your ass. And that is a threat." She lowers her voice as she gets into my face.

I hold my breath because I am scared that if I inhale her scent, I won't be able to let her away from me again. I nod my head because I am heady from her proximity and I cannot think straight. She glares at me for a moment longer before stepping away from me. As she starts walking away from me once more, I finally snap out of my daze.

"Do you want me to give you a ride to the party?" I ask, forgetting completely that I am trying to keep professional relations with her in front of my friends. She is just someone who is living in my house and paying me rent for. The same goes for my friends, not that they really care about what happens in my life, as long as it doesn't involve them.

"No, I will find a way there," she calls back, not looking at me. I have half a mind to plead with her or demand that she come with me, but I keep my mouth shut, lest I offend her again. I watch as she walks out of the front gate and disappears around the corner. Once she is gone, I get into my own car and start the engine, pulling out of the driveway.

Tonight might not have been my ideal Friday night, but now, I am a little more excited to go to the party than I was before, and the reason has just stormed out of the property wearing pants and a shirt, a simple outfit, but one that has me falling in love with her all over again.

***

I scan the living room, pulsating with music, searching for a head of red hair and green eyes that seem to pierce through mine every time I look into them, but in vain. The four hours that I've been at the party, all I've been doing, was searching for Madeline.

I try so hard not to think about her, to enjoy myself and focus on my friends who are joking around me, but I can't. All I can think of is her. I want to see her again. I can't talk to her in front of my friends, of course, but I still want to look at her. A glimpse would do.

"Where is your head at, Steven?" Gia asks, brushing her fingers along my arm. I glance at her as I take a sip of my beer, shaking my head.

"Nothing," I lie as my eyes start their search once more.

"Are you looking for someone?" She asks, leaning forward as if we are sharing a secret. After the stunt in the cafeteria the other day with Madeline, I've been feeling this strange disgust and repulsion toward her. I can't bring myself to look at her without feeling angry all over again, much less talking to her.

"Yes, I am," I answer because I want her off my back. I don't want to be her little boy toy tonight. Or any other night. In my freshman year, I would have jumped at the chance to sleep with Gia, but I've lost my interest in her, because now I know what kind of person she really is.

"Oh, who's that lucky girl?" She asks, pouting a little. I peel my gaze away from her, glancing at my friends. But none of them are looking at me. They are all engrossed in conversation or maybe trying to avoid Gia like I am. She hangs out with our group a lot, but none of the guys really like her.

We have discussed our mutual dislike for her more than once.

"I need another beer," I push away from the counter we were leaning against and walk away from Gia, disregarding her question completely. I know that maybe my group is the only one that is immune to Gia's hate and her scorn. I am secretly glad of it because she can be a crazy bitch. I usually let her stay with us, talk to us, and be friendly to her lest she tries to turn her psychotic side on us, but tonight, I don't want to hear her or tolerate her.

I swig another drink from my almost empty beer bottle as I head for the kitchen to get another. I want to be drunk tonight. Maybe it will make me feel a little better. Maybe that is all I need to loosen up and have a good time. I don't notice the person coming out of the kitchen as I make my way inside until I run into them and my beer bottle slipping from my fingers and crashing on the floor. What the heck?!

***

CHAPTER THIRTEEN

Madeline Scott

I don't think I have ever felt more frustrated by Steven than I do tonight. First, he annoyed me by calling me a stereotypical nerd back at the house. And now he has run, and smashed into my chest, spilling my drink all over my pants. Thankfully, I chose to wear the dark ones tonight, or I would have gone psycho on him.

"What on earth is wrong with you?" I ask him

as he stumbles away from me. Emma, who walks out after me, grabs my arm at my words.

"It's okay, honey. We will clean you up. Come on," she says, her voice soft. I don't budge from where I stand, glaring at the soccer captain in front of me. I know I am not exactly the most qualified person to be talking so rudely to the man in front of me, all according to the people currently present in this house, but I am a little tipsy, and my tongue has gone loose. Apparently, my temper has risen too.

"I am so sorry, Maddy—" Steven begins but stops abruptly, as if realizing that the others don't know that we are on a nickname basis.

"You ruined my pants. My favorite pants!" That's an exaggeration because these are definitely not my favorite pants, but I am in the mood for war. Or maybe drunk Maddy is.

"I said I am sorry," he grits out, getting annoyed with me too. He doesn't get to be angry with me. He doesn't get to be frustrated with me when he was the one who ran into me.

"Oh, of course, you are. A soccer god like you can do no wrong and is asking for my forgiveness nonetheless," I sigh dramatically. I am being an ass, but the anger from earlier returns in full force. "I don't accept your apology," I press my lips into a tight line.

"Maddy, let's go. We need to clean you up. It's okay. He didn't see you," Emma tries to console me, but I settle my glare on her. Lenny walks up to us then, and I watch as Emma turns to look at him.

"Maddy, come on. Let's go," he says to me, his tone matching Em's. I don't know what it is with them talking to me like I am a child. I am vaguely aware of everyone's eyes on me, but I am not in the mood to care. I was mad when I got to the party and had a few drinks, to try and kill the annoyance I felt. Now that I am properly drunk, I am no closer to letting go of my grudge toward Steven.

"It's you again," someone snaps, and I glance at Steven's side to find a five-foot-five-inch-tall menace. She calls herself Gia. "Is she troubling you, Steven?" she asks her friend, but he doesn't say anything. His gaze is fixed on me as if I am a puzzle he is trying to solve. Or as if he wants to strangle me.

"Aww, are you here to help out little baby Steven? Are you his mommy?" I ask, anger flaring until it fills every pore of my being.

Gia's face turns red with anger. Steven stares at me with a hint of anger in his eyes, but he doesn't say anything as I take a step closer to Gia.

Emma's grip on my arm tightens, but I yank it out of her grip. She lets me go, taking a step toward her boyfriend.

"Walking around acting like you own the place or a person doesn't mean that you actually do. Stay out of this or else—" Before I can finish the sentence, Gia gets in my face, her eyes wild.

"Or else what? Are you threatening me, wannabe?" She asks. The insult unleashes every bit of self-control that was restraining me till now.

"Gia." Before I can open my mouth to shower her with the choice words I have picked out for her in my head, Steven intervenes. His voice is firm, and he grabs Gia's arm, pulling her away from me. "That's enough. She is drunk. Let her be," he adds.

"I am not drunk," I defend myself even as I sway on my feet as I move. Emma is by my side once again, her arms holding me in place. I lean against her hold and point at the people in front of me. "Tell them I am not drunk," I tell her.

"Yes, I will tell them. But right now, we have to go, okay? You need to sleep it off," she responds, trying to veer me away from Steven and Gia. I stay rooted to my spot, glaring at the two.

"Of course, she is not drunk. She is just as weird when she is sober. Walking around with a smile on her face, talking to everyone and anyone, being a social butterfly as if people can stand her presence for even a moment. She is not drunk, you guys. She is just a weird hippie bitch," Gia chuckles, announcing the words to the crowd that has gathered around us.

At some point, the music stopped so her voice could be heard loud and clear. I grit my teeth as I try to not launch myself at her and rip the hair out of her head. I glance at Steven, vaguely remembering him telling me that he is not like the people he hangs out with. He just tries to get Gia away from me but doesn't defend me, doesn't tell her that she is the one who is being a bitch to me.

I smirk at him. Jock. I don't know why I ever thought of him as different from the rest. I don't know why I let myself romanticize the idea of him and convince myself that he is better than the others, that he isn't stuck up or disrespectful like the others. But he is just the same, if not worse, than the others.

I take a step away from Gia and Steven then, glancing at the former with a warning in my eyes.

"Weird hippie bitch, huh? Try to come up with something more creative. No wonder the art club kicked your ass out," I spit out, watching as her expression turns thunderous.

But before she can say anything, Emma makes me walk away from her, right to the front door and out onto the porch. I know it was a low blow to call her out on the one disaster she had endured at the university, and I am not one to broadcast other people's flaws in public, but this was my last straw.

She was pressing on every one of my nerves, and I snapped.

"She is going to kill you, you know," Emma mumbles in my ear as she guides me down the steps of the porch and toward a car that I recognize as Lenny's. As if on cue, her boyfriend appears on my other side, unlocking the vehicle. My best friend gently helps me into the back seat as Lenny walks to the driver's seat.

Emma joins me in the back, even though she usually sits in the front with him. I don't complain as she wraps her arms around me. I lay my head on her shoulder and close my eyes because I suddenly feel very tired.

My eyelids grow heavy, and through the fog in my mind, I recall Gia's words, the way she spoke them, the confidence with which she said them. None of it was true. I know it in my heart, but I can't help the way my chin wobbles, and I feel as if a dam is about to break.

"A weird hippie bitch," I murmur to Emma, not caring that Lenny can hear everything from the front seat. "She called me weird and a bitch." I don't take "hippie" as an insult, even though I am not one, but I do take "weird" and "bitch" as one.

I have thick skin, but sometimes insults penetrate through it and stab me right in the heart. I am only human, after all.

"You are not any of those things. You are my

sweet, amazing Maddy who loves to make friends and put a smile on people's faces," Emma replies, and I shake my head.

A teardrop falls onto my cheek, and I want to push it right back in. I want to undo this process because I don't like to be sad. I like to be happy always. Even when I feel like the world is ending, I like to be smiling and dancing around.

"She meant it," I say, my voice full of tears. I feel Emma's arms wrapping tighter around my body.

"She is the bitch. Not you." She kisses the top of my head as I begin crying then.

I bury my face in my arms, and I break down completely. I don't want to hold back. It might be the alcohol, or it might be the years of pent-up frustration and sadness. My life is not perfect, even though I like to act like it is. Pretending that everything is fine is just a coping mechanism. Or perhaps it is a mental condition. I don't really care because I would rather not feel the way that I am feeling right now.

"Do you want to stay with me tonight?" Emma asks, and I nod my head. I don't want to go back to the house. I don't think it is a good idea for me to be in the same space as Steven right now.

I am afraid I might take my anger out on him, even though he deserves some of it.

"I want to stay with you all the time," I say to my best friend. She chuckles as she squeezes me affectionately.

"Same," she responds, and I feel myself cracking a smile through my tears. This is better. More me.

"I feel left out," Lenny comments from the driver's seat, and Emma and I burst out laughing.

"It's okay. She's your girlfriend. You can have her, too," I reply to him, feeling generous. I would rather not share Emma with anyone, but she can have a boyfriend. She deserves to be happy.

"Thank you so much, ma'am," Lenny responds. I glance at the rearview mirror to find him grinning at me. I return the gesture, internally cringing at the way my eye makeup has dissolved with the tears and is now running down my face.

"I survived the party for four hours," I tell Emma. I was so mad when I arrived that I wasn't sure I could keep my fury in for more than thirty seconds. Four hours is impressive.

"Yes, you did. Good job," my best friend praises me, and pride fills my chest for no apparent reason. I am glad for the veil of alcohol over my senses at the moment. I doubt that I would feel like smiling again so soon, if it weren't for the liquor running through my body.

Lenny pulls into the dorm's parking lot, and we get out of the car. I stumble over my own feet twice before my friends decide that it is best if I am carried to the room. Lenny picks me up and begins walking, Emma by his side. I feel weird in his arms because it feels wrong to me. I don't want Emma to be offended by me or be mad at me.

I know I am being irrational, and she will never doubt me, but you never know. I try to swallow my protests, though because I am fully aware that I will faceplant if I attempt to walk on my own. Thankfully, the trip to Emma's room is short and sweet. I heave a sigh of relief as Lenny puts me down on my best friend's bed, where I promptly pass out the moment my head touches the pillow.

***

CHAPTER FOURTEEN

Steven Jones

I arrive at the house early in the morning, my head pounding from the drinks I consumed all night. I kill the engine, exit the car, and enter the house. The foyer is dimly lit by the early morning sunlight seeping through the open front door. I listen for any sounds but hear none. Did Madeline not come home last night? Or maybe she is still asleep. What do I care anyway?

I sigh as I close the front door and head towards my room, but not before pausing outside Madeline's room, which is down the hall from mine. No sounds come from the other side, and I straighten. I know it's a breach of her privacy, but I can't help but wonder if she got home safely after the scene at the party.

I don't know how I feel about last night, after what happened with Gia and Madeline. On one hand, I feel like Gia crossed a few lines and hurt Madeline. But on the other hand, I am mad at Madeline for treating me with such hatred. It seemed that she didn't actually accept my apology earlier in the evening before we left for the party.

Opening the door to her room, I peek inside only to find it bathed in soft morning light. It is empty otherwise, with no sign of Madeline. I frown, wondering if she went to her friend's dorm. I shake my head, forcing myself to step out of the room. So much for not caring.

Madeline is not a little girl, I have to remind myself. She can take care of herself, and I don't need to coddle her. She can deal with her own problems and emotions. She is more than capable of doing so.

Last night, after she left the party, Gia went around seeking sympathy from everyone she could find. She made the whole incident seem like a fresh show starring Madeline. None of the people at the party tried to defend Maddy or tell Gia that she was being harsh to her.

I stayed out of the drama because I didn't want to slip up and take Madeline's side by accident. I don't want people getting the wrong idea. It would be the right idea technically, but I don't want them finding out that I like Madeline, that I like her as a friend, as a person, as a partner.

Even after how she treated me last night, I can't let go of my feelings for her. I did feel angry toward her, but it was partly my fault, too, making her feel like crap earlier. Holding a grudge is on her, but I don't think she was in the right frame of mind last night, so that I could try and explain it to her.

I drag a hand through my hair as I walk into my room and try to relax a little. My friends laughed at Madeline's audacity last night, saying that she seemed to be growing claws and that they couldn't wait to see her get into a catfight with Gia. I don't know how two people fighting with each other is remotely entertaining, but I'm not going to question the jocks.

I've been a part of the community long enough to know that a lot of things that jocks do, doesn't make sense in the least. They like things just for the sake of it or just because other people don't. I peel my shirt over my head and toss it into the laundry basket as I head to the bathroom for a much-needed shower. Maybe I'll call Madeline afterward and ask her if she's okay.

But before I can go through with my plans, my phone rings. I glance at the screen, and my throat dries up when I see my father's Caller ID flashing across the screen. Shit.

I haven't talked to my parents in a few days, mostly because Madeline had been around quite a lot, and I didn't want her accidentally walking into the room or talking to me while I was on the phone with them. I know that I am going to get an earful for being careless and not keeping in touch with them.

I contemplate letting the call go to voicemail, but I know my father will be doubly pissed later that I am not up at the crack of dawn. Swallowing a groan, I reach forward and pick up my phone, answering the call. I put the call on speaker since I am home alone and move to my bed to tidy the room up while I am talking to my father.

"Good morning, Dad." I try to sound as cheerful as possible even though I don't feel half as excited as I am trying to be.

"Good morning. Where have you been?" He asks, and I wince slightly. Shit. "You haven't called in four days, Steven. Your mom and I are worried for you. You know you should reach out to us regularly and keep us updated about soccer and your studies. How can you be so irresponsible?" He adds.

There is that word again, the one I hate. I don't know how my father uses it with such ease, with such nonchalance and indifference. I don't know how he can bear to call his only son irresponsible when I have given up my life, just to please him.

I run in the circles that I do because my father approves of my friends. He wants me to be friends with guys like me, as if he knows what kind of a person I am. He never once tried to even ask me what I was interested in for fuck's sake. I love soccer. I truly do. But somewhere I feel like I only love it and put so much time and energy into it because my father wants me to.

"I have been busy with assignments, Dad. Coach has been keeping us longer for practice these days, and I am trying to keep up with the classes so I don't fall back on my grades." I respond. It is not a lie. I have been awfully busy the past few days. I have been juggling schoolwork and soccer and going batshit crazy trying to do both, for real.

"I think you can still find some time for your

parents," my father snaps, and I straighten. My muscles tense, and I want to ask him to leave me alone. I want to ask him what he expects of me now. I am tired of giving, but I know I can't afford to stop because what will I even do, who will I even be if I stop listening to my father, if I stop living for him?

"I am sorry. I will be more careful from now on," I reply, knowing that this is the answer he wants. I have a feeling that my father loves to hear me apologize for things. I feel like he likes to see me be apologetic and sad over him. I can't fathom why for the life of me, but it seems to be the case.

"I expect you to be regular with your calls," my father simply says before diving into business right away. He asks me about my soccer practice and if I scored any goals during the practice matches. I tell him that I did, and then he goes on to tell me that he went through my grades again since the dean sent him an overview of my performance.

I listen raptly as I clean my room. I can very well zone him out, but I don't dare to because I know that at any given moment he will ask me something, and I won't be able to answer him. I have lived with my parents long enough to know their likes and dislikes. I know their tricks and what makes them want to disown me. I have cataloged it all over the years, so now it is easy for me to not get in trouble. Well, most of the time. Sometimes, it is just inevitable.

When my father finally lets me get off the phone, the sun has fully risen, and my room is bathed in warm, bright light. My head still throbs in pain behind my eyes, so I sit down on my bed and chase down an Advil with water, trying to get rid of the reminder of just how many drinks I had last night.

I usually don't drink, mostly because of soccer. I don't like putting substances into my body that might hamper my techniques, my strength, etc. But yesterday, I think I deserved it after the long day that I have had. I glance at the alarm clock on my nightstand, only to find that it is seven in the morning.

Damn, my father and I were on the phone for the past two hours. That's new. And what is even more surprising is that in the two hours we talked, not once did he ask me how I was doing, if things were okay with me, if I was overwhelmed with my studies since this is my last year.

I shake my head at myself, chiding myself for thinking that my father would coddle me, wanting to know about my well-being. As long as my grades don't drop and he doesn't think I am lacking in soccer, he doesn't feel the need to ask me about me. Even when he does, his words usually insinuate that something is wrong with me and I should just get out of my head and get back in the game.

This has resulted in me disregarding my own feelings over the years. It is crazy how others treat you, affecting your own view of yourself. I don't think even I know most of the time, about how I am feeling. When I am feeling down, I tell myself that I will be fine and that it will pass. It is as if my brain reigns over my heart most of the time, shadowing the parts of me I want to reach but can't because there is too much darkness surrounding it.

I get up from my bed and walk over to my desk to get my phone. I want to make the call that I wanted to make after taking my shower. I think I should just call Madeline now, just in case I get distracted yet again after I get out of the shower.

I dial her number and pace the length of the

room, waiting for her to pick up. I have never seen her wasted before, and seeing her drunk last night intrigued me as much as it scared me. She didn't give a fuck about all the people who were surrounding her. She didn't care that the woman she was talking to, standing up to, could very well get her kicked out of the university if she was even slightly pissed off.

Madeline seemed to only want to protect herself, save herself. And I am impressed by her guts. Yes, she pissed me off, but the rest of the interaction had been about Gia, and I had enjoyed every moment of it. Perhaps because I can't think of ever standing up to Gia like the way Madeline did. I can't imagine being so brave, so bold that I challenge the woman who has all the students wrapped around her pinky finger.

"Hello?" A raspy, female voice says into the speaker, and I focus on the present once again.

"Maddy?" I ask, letting loose a breath that I didn't realize I have been holding.

"Yes. Why are you calling me at seven in the morning, Steven?" She questions, a pause following it.

"I wanted to check up on you. I came home, and you weren't here, so I thought I would call you and see if you were okay," I answer, massaging the back of my neck. She makes me so nervous, dammit.

"I am fine. I crashed at Emma's dorm room. I will see you soon," she half mumbles before the line goes dead. I am not offended because it seemed that she was still half asleep. I smile as I pull the device from the ear. At least, she seemed to have forgotten about what happened last night.

***

CHAPTER FIFTEEN

MADELINE SCOTT

My hangover is a menace. I groan as I massage my temples, propped up against the headboard of Emma's bed. I can't even bring myself to open my eyes, and my stomach is doing somersaults. I am never drinking again.

"I told you to take it slow." Emma's voice, too loud for my liking, scolds me as she settles on the edge of the bed next to me. "Drink this. You will feel better."

I glance at her hand reluctantly to find that she has brought me a steaming cup of hot coffee. I could kiss her right now if it weren't for the fact that, I surely will faint if I move too quickly.

"Thank you so much. You are a lifesaver." I manage to croak out as I take the coffee cup from her hands and take a sip. The bitter taste of coffee melts on my tongue and stings the back of my throat, but it is a welcome discomfort. I can't imagine how I would survive in a world where there is no coffee or Emma.

"Last night was a shitshow, huh?" Emma asks, her voice taking on a nervous tone. I glance at her with a frown settled between my brows.

"What do you mean?" I can't really remember everything that happened except for me and Gia getting into a fight. I don't remember what was said and if anyone was hurt. Physically.

"Getting into an argument with Gia is my definition of a shitshow. And landing the last blow to her ego is my definition of a fuck-up." My best friend points out before going on to recall the whole incident to me. By the time she finishes, I am mentally facepalming myself. I don't like Gia, but I try not to mess with her too much because she can make my life a living hell. God, what have I done?

"She deserved it, but I know, I should have been more careful." I answer. I will not say that Gia didn't deserve to be put in her rightful place, but I could have handled the situation a little bit more maturely. "Well, she is going to kill me now." I sigh, my shoulders sagging.

I am not too scared of Gia because I have pissed her off plenty of times before and she hasn't done anything major other than turning her bitchiness on me up a notch. But I prefer to not go around broadcasting my dislike for her.

"You should have just left with me when I asked

you to." Emma nods her head in agreement. "It was nice knowing you, Madeline Scott. If something happens to you, I will take care of your makeup collection." She adds.

"Nothing is going to happen to me. I will be fine. And I have been dealing with Gia for the past three years. I have seen all her colors. I doubt I have anything else left to witness." I shrug, trying to act nonchalant.

In reality, I cannot stop thinking about what Gia will do to me now. The little bitch can pull elaborate stunts without getting into trouble ever, and I have seen students crying and leaving university just because she became too much for them to handle. But that's not me, though. I am Madeline Scott, aka Maddy. Bitches don't scare me....Well, to a certain extent, they don't.

"I didn't like how Steven stood by her side, instead of yours. He should have been the one carrying you to my room, the one defending you in a room full of suckers," Emma's words snap me out of my worries.

I'm going to be fine. I'm just paranoid, that's it. I tell myself.

"Why would he defend me when he is friends with Gia?" I ask my best friend because her logic doesn't make sense. I'm not really mad at Steven for not standing up for me, because I came to the realization last night that he wasn't different after all, he was just like the other jocks.

It's best if I eliminate my feelings for him and move on. This is the right time to do so, since my annoyance and disheartened feelings toward him are still fresh.

"Gia was being a bitch. It doesn't matter that she is his friend. If you ever speak to or speak of another person the way Gia talks about you and the other students, I would have unfriended you a long time ago," she replies, playing with her hands on her lap.

"I would never treat people the way she treats me," I remind Emma because she seems to have forgotten that I don't particularly get off on hurting other people. It's not my field of expertise, and I don't find any enjoyment in it either.

"I know, Maddy. I was giving you an example, that's all," Emma consoles me. I nod my head, pursing my lips in distaste.

"Anyway, can we not talk about Steven or Gia? My headache is getting worse," I massage my temple, draining the last bit of my coffee.

"What do you want to talk about then?" Emma asks, and I know that there is going to be a gossip session that follows her tone of voice. I'm not complaining, though. I sit eagerly as I wait for her to spill the latest tea.

The only good thing that comes from going to a party is that you get to know about a lot of people, especially when you're around loosened tongues because of alcohol.

***

I look around the theater room, the students having left after our practice. I sit on the stage, going through my lines again. I know them by memory now, but I can't help but feel paranoid that I will mess up on the big day. I know that it's just me getting cold feet and experiencing nerves, but I cannot shake it off.

I replay today's practice over in my head, going over every little scene, every little line. The play seems to be going smoothly, and the characters are playing their part exceptionally, so then, why am I scared?

I turn on my phone to check the time and find it is quite late. I need to get to the house. I won't get a ride if I don't leave right now. I get up from the stage and collect my things, walking out of the theater room once I have made sure that all the lights are off.

I walk into the parking lot of the campus to find one single car idling around. The rest of the parking lot is empty, and I quicken my steps to get the hell out of the place. I don't like isolated places. No, let me rephrase that. I don't like isolated places at night when no one is around and anything can happen to me.

I am not too keen to be killed just yet. Pulling my phone out of my pocket, I put Emma's number on speed dial. I don't want to take any risks. I know I am just letting my fears get the best of me, and the chances are that the car belongs to one of the faculty members or a student like me, but I prefer to be cautious.

A shadow moves somewhere behind the car, and I freeze. My legs refuse to cooperate with my brain as the shadow moves again, the sound of concrete crunching under the person's footsteps the only sound audible in the empty parking lot.

I have half a mind to call out to the person and ask them what they are doing here, but my tongue seems to be stuck to the roof of my mouth, my throat going dry. The shadow steps out from behind the car and begins walking toward me.

My heart thunders in my chest as I realize that the person has probably seen me too.

I will myself to turn around and run into the building, but my legs are frozen in place. I stare at the approaching figure, wondering if this is how I will meet my end. What a tragic way to die! People will know about my death. They will assume things, and even in death, I won't have peace.

I find my voice as soon as the figure gets within five feet of me. "If you take another step forward, I am calling the police!" I shriek, my voice high-pitched and scared.

The figure stares at me, not responding. I doubt they will be scared by an empty threat of the police if they are a skilled kidnapper or murderer.

"I am not joking. I will call the police and then kick your ass," I repeat as I take a step away from them. The figure shakes its head, and I realize that they are probably not scared of the police or me.

"See, I am going to scream at the top of my lungs if you don't leave me alone right at this moment," I add, gritting my teeth.

My insides are in turmoil, and my heart is racing a mile a minute. "Madeline—" The figure starts, and my head rears back in shock.

"How do you know my name?" My heart is beating in my ear, and I have never heard it beat so loud and so fast.

"Because I am Steven," the figure responds, pulling the hood of the jacket he is wearing back from his face. My mouth falls open, and relief floods through my chest as I realize that the person in front of me is not a killer but my roommate.

"What are you doing here?" I ask him, letting go of my fear and taking a step toward him. I can see his face now under the dim lamp in one corner of the parking lot. Embarrassment comes to meet me, and I want to disappear into thin air.

"I came here to pick you up, since you were late,"

he replies, looking around the parking lot. "I was wondering if I did the wrong thing, but now I see this was the right thing to do since you are so bad at trying to scare off potential kidnappers," he adds, chuckling a little.

My cheeks burn as I walk past him toward his car, trying to ignore the fact that he drove all the way here to pick me up. I am not sure how to feel about it. Every time I try to push my feelings for him away, he does something that has my heart sighing and melting in my chest.

"I tried my best. And I was caught by surprise, okay?" I huff as he falls into step beside me.

"Of course, of course," Steven nods, his voice teasing. "A gangster will give you a heads-up for sure before attacking you."

"Ass," I mutter under my breath but get into the passenger seat of the car anyway. I am not going to be a brat and be stubborn when I have had one scare already.

"Do you really think threatening to kick someone's ass will get him to leave you alone?" Steven asks, his laugh reverberating through the car as he starts the engine and pulls out of the parking lot. He is never going to let me live it down, is he?

***

CHAPTER SIXTEEN

Steven Jones

As the days pass by and Madeline continues to live in the house, I find myself becoming more attracted to her than before. She is a force of nature. She is unapologetic. She is brave. She doesn't care about what others say about her, or at least she pretends that she doesn't.

She is the person I wish I could be, and I feel myself falling for her a little more every day.

She never fails to put a smile on my face. I don't remember smiling so much, in a very long time. She has a way about her, a carefree, happy demeanor that just puts me at ease, every time she is around. Especially the way she doesn't really mind telling people exactly what she thinks of them.

I smile to myself as I pour cereal into my bowl, followed by some milk. I sit in the dining room alone, having my breakfast, before I need to leave for early morning practice. I have another practice in the evening, and I am not looking forward to either of them. I am tired and sore all over from yesterday's practice, and all I want to do is curl up in bed and sleep.

But if I skip practice, chances are that the coach will call my father and let him know that his son has not come to practice today, which will be followed by a lecture from my father about how irresponsible I am and how I will never make it big if I keep skipping practices.

The smile that I had been sporting slips right off my face. I swallow a few choice words that come to my mind every time I realize how my life is not really mine. Before I can dwell too much on how miserable I am with my life, the door to the dining room opens, and Madeline walks in with a plate in one hand and a glass of orange juice in the other.

She walks over to the table and takes a seat in her usual chair across from me. "Good morning," she mumbles as she digs into her breakfast of bacon and eggs. I watch her eat, wondering where she gets the motivation to make herself breakfast. I prefer to eat cereal most mornings because it's quick and tasty.

"Good morning," I respond as I continue

shoveling spoonful of milk and cereal into my mouth. I should not be having so much sugar, but the supermarket was out of the cereal that I usually buy, a low-fat, no-sugar one, so I have to settle for this. Honestly, this is so much better than the no-added sugar stuff that I usually eat. I might just permanently switch to this one.

"Can I ask you something?" Madeline asks out of the blue, making me look at her. It's not unusual for her to be up this early because some days she has practice, and others, she just wakes up early to go to the cafe.

"Yes, go ahead," I gesture for her to ask, and she looks around the room before speaking.

"I don't mean to pry, but I've been living here for four weeks now, and not once have I seen you invite people over. I mean, it's a little weird that you don't even invite your friends over," she says, her eyes still scanning her surroundings.

I force my cereal down my throat as I try to come up with a reason, an excuse to tell her. I rub the back of my neck, a tic I want to get rid of because of how obvious it is, as I rack my brain for something to say. In the end, I find nothing, so I settle on the truth.

"My parents don't like me having people over in the house." I don't tell her the part where they think that bringing friends over to the house is crossing boundaries and it will do nothing but make me a failure.

Madeline blinks at me as if surprised. "Really? That's… interesting." She takes a bite of her eggs, her gaze searching my face in that way that only she can look at people. It is as if she is trying to put a puzzle together, and every time she stares at me that way, she seems satisfied when she is done.

"Yes, I don't mind it though, because I don't even really like-" I stop abruptly, realizing what I was about to say, what I almost revealed. I backtrack, trying to turn the words around and hoping that my slip-up goes unnoticed, even though it was quite obvious.

"How come they allowed me to stay here then?" She asks, and I am glad that she doesn't push me, doesn't ask me about my sudden silence.

"They don't know about you." I respond truthfully once again. Madeline's fork almost slips out of her hands, and a look passes over her expression before it stays.

"What do you mean they don't know about me?" She asks, her expression horrified.

I feel embarrassed about telling her why I haven't told my parents about her staying at the house, but I don't want to give birth to distrust between us.

"My parents will kick you out if they know that I am not the only one occupying this house. I didn't tell them about the arrangement because I know they would never say yes to it." I confess. Madeline's eyes widen, and she shakes her head as if in disbelief.

"So, you mean to say that your parents are unaware of my presence in this house. I am living here in secret?" It seems as if she is wheezing. I don't know why she sounded so panicked. It is okay. As long as my parents don't show up at my front doorstep, there is no way they will know about Madeline.

"I am not that close with my parents, Maddy. And I don't know how to talk to them about me feeling quite lonely in this house all by myself. I know it seems as though I am being ungrateful, but living in a house this big, without friends, without someone to talk to, to spend time with, gets lonely. I have been… depressed for the past few months, and that is why when I saw that you needed a place to live, I asked you to come live with me." I explain to her in a rush, hoping that she understands.

"But not telling your parents about the arrangement is kind of stupid. What if they find out from someone else? It would be a disaster." She reasons, but her voice has calmed down. Her tone has turned gentle, and there is sadness in her eyes for me. No pity. No sympathy. Only a quiet sadness.

"I know they will freak out if they find out from someone else, but nobody else close to them knows either. There is no way that word will get around to them. My friends don't really care about what goes on in my personal life. They don't even know that I don't particularly have a relationship with my parents," I say, stirring my cereal, just to have something to do.

Madeline is quiet for a long moment after my confession. I feel her gaze on me, but I don't dare to look at her. I am afraid of what I will find in her eyes, this time. The sadness I can handle, but I don't think I am capable of handling any other emotion from her.

"But friends are supposed to know you, Steve. Every part of you. Even the parts you hate," she says gently, and I shrug, a self-deprecating smile making its way onto my face. "Do you not talk to your friends about yourself? What do you talk to them about then?" She asks.

"This is the first time I have ever told anybody how things with my parents really are. Everyone expects me to be this carefree, happy, playboy jock who doesn't have a care in the world. They expect me to have every happiness in the world just because my parents are rich. They expect me to never shed a tear, never be sad because it wouldn't fit into the role they want me to play." I glance up at Madeline finally to find her listening intently.

"I don't talk to my friends about myself. Never before have I dared to talk to them about my life, my problems, because I tried in the beginning, but they shut me out. I like my friends. I do, even though I don't agree with everything they do, or maybe because they are the only ones I have. But I don't feel a connection to them. I don't feel like I can lay myself bare in front of them, and expect that they will protect me, hide me," I confess.

A weight lifts off my shoulders at the admission. I feel freer than I did before, and I feel a breath of relief leaving my chest. I feel the hollow space in my heart being filled slightly, as if I have healed it. I don't know what this feeling is and how long it will last, but I am not ready to let go of it.

"Why are you telling me all of this?" Madeline asks, her voice unsure. I smile as I look at her, shrugging.

"I don't know. Maybe because I know you are someone who values emotions. Maybe because I know that you value friendship, secrets, heartbreaks, and love. Maybe because you are the only one who ever makes me want to smile. Maybe because you have that energy about you that makes people feel comfortable in your presence and breathe a little more freely," I reply.

"So, you don't think I am a weird hippie bitch?" Madeline raise an eyebrow at me, and I wince.

"I am sorry that Gia called you that. I don't

agree with her, and I doubt even she agrees with herself. But you are the truest person I have met, Maddy. I don't know why I never befriended you before, but I am glad we met," I say truthfully. I didn't feel like I had to pretend around her. The jock refused to make an appearance in her presence.

"Aww, I am flattered, Jones," she grins at me, and that grin made me feel relaxed enough to let up another smile.

"I really hoped that I could tell my parents about someone living in the house with me, but I can't. They have been calling me, but I have not been picking up their video calls in case you walk into the frame or speak when I am on a call," I admit sheepishly.

"Oh my God. You can just tell me when you are talking to them, and I will keep my mouth shut.

Contrary to popular opinion, I can keep quiet," she answer her, and I laugh. She laughs with me, and I feel much, much lighter than before.

"Also, Steve," Madeline says, a moment later.

"Yes?" I ask, tilting my head to the side slightly.

"I am sorry for everything that happened at the party. I was rude to you, and I shouldn't have been. I was being a bitch for no reason at all," she smile ruefully, and I wave her off, even though a flood of relief fills me up once again.

"It's okay. We were both bitches to each other," I shake my head.

"That is true. I am not usually that short-tempered. I think I was just stressed and had one too many drinks," she chews on her bottom lip.

"It's okay to lose your temper at times, Maddy. It makes us human," I tell her, and she nods her head.

"And sharing our emotions and feelings makes us human, too," she responds, and I swear I could feel myself falling for her a little more in that moment.

***

CHAPTER SEVENTEEN

Madeline Scott

"How is life, Maddy?" Dad asks as he leans back in his recliner, my mother trying to get in the frame from beside him.

"Pretty good. Two days later, we have our show, and I am nervous but very, very excited too," I tell him, and he grins. My mother continues to struggle to get into the frame.

"That sounds exciting. Are you guys prepared

for the big day? I am sure you will be great," he says, and I grin. I am sure we will do great. I am not trying to sound vain, just hopeful and a little delusional. I am trying to manifest the success of our show.

"Are you still living with the soccer boy?" My mother asks, and my gaze flickers over to Steven, who is sitting on the living room couch across from me.

He cocks an eyebrow at me, making me look away, a blush spreading across my cheeks.

"Yes, mom. And his name is Steven," I respond to my mother, who rolls her eyes.

"Whatever. I still don't think it is a good idea or appropriate for a Christian woman to be living with a man who isn't her father, brother, or husband," my mother mutters, and I feel myself wanting to be swallowed whole by the floor. Why is she like this?

"Are you eating your meals on time, Maddy?" My father asks, and I nod my head, too embarrassed to say anything. I can feel Steven looking at me. I want to tell him to stop staring and walk out of the room before my mother blurts out something more that can humiliate me more.

"Who cooks the food? You or the…soccer guy?" My mother intervenes into the conversation once more. Okay, this is getting out of hand now.

"We cook our own meals, mom. And what kind of a question is that? I am eating. I am healthy. I am thriving," I answer, adamant about making her let go of the soccer guy sitting across from me. When I dare a glance at Steven, I find him sitting back on the couch with his arms behind his head, listening to my conversation with great interest.

"Did you sleep with him, Madeline?" My mother's question sends my heart plummeting to the pit of my stomach. One corner of Steven's lips twitches up in an amused smirk at my reaction, which portrays exactly what I am feeling.

"Mom!" I cry as I look back at the screen. "Of course not! And you can't go around asking me if I have slept with a guy. That is my business," I add, feeling annoyed now. I don't usually get annoyed with my mother, but she has been acting crazy ever since I moved in with Steven.

My father gives me an apologetic look as he turns to my mother. "You are making her uncomfortable, honey. She is a big girl. I think she can make her own decision, although I would prefer it if no man ever touches her." He glances at me as he says the last part.

My cheeks turned red, and I feel as if I am

going to explode. Why did I think it was a good idea to attend a call from my parents while I was in the living room with Steven? I don't know, but I am regretting my decision with every passing moment.

"I will talk to you guys later, when you realize that you can't go around asking people if they are sleeping around with every guy they are in a room with. Good bye," I gritted out and ended the call, letting out a groan as I let my head fall back against the couch. I closed my eyes, not wanting to look at Steven. Maybe if I pretended that nothing happened, then this interaction would undo itself.

Slowly, I opened my eyes only to find Steven right in front of me. His arms were braced against the armrests of the couch, and he was leaning forward, his eyes boring into mine. My breath catches in my throat, and I feel myself getting flushed all over. Is it okay for him to be this close to me? Do roommates look so smug...and sexy all the time?

"I'm sorry you had to hear that," I mumble, making myself smile a little, as if the conversation was not a big deal and I wasn't freaking out.

"Your mother thinks that we are sleeping together?" Steven asks, and I swallow a whimper. I didn't want to make a fool of myself. I would never forgive my mother for putting me in this position.

"She's just scared that I might sleep around with guys and lose my virginity. Little does she know, it's already lost," I blurt out before I realize just how unnecessary the information is.

I clamp my mouth shut, mentally facepalming myself. I want to slam my head against a wall and be done with it.

Steven's eyes searches my face, and his expression darken. I didn't know why he looks at me that way, but it made my skin tingle, and my heart leaps in my chest, steadily and rapidly.

"Who did you lose it to?" He asks, and I almost choked on my own saliva. What is that supposed to mean?

"Excuse me?" I ask, frowning. I didn't know if it is appropriate for us to be having this conversation. I didn't know if roommates usually discussed such topics. Did our arrangement include this?

"I want to know who it was that got to be your first," He says, his eyes boring into mine as if he could see right through me.

"Why?" I ask, but my voice feels nothing more than a whisper. He smirks once again, making me blush once more. I didn't know what this conversation is and why we were having it in the first place, but suddenly I feel hot all over, and my heart was racing like I had just run a marathon.

"I want to know. In case I ever see him," He answers. I didn't know what to make of his response. I am too nervous to ask him about it. I just stare back at him, wondering if the air was always so thick, every time he was around me.

A ringtone pierces through the air, and Steven straightens, blinking several times as if coming up from a dream. I look away from him as he makes his way back to the couch and picks up his phone. I watch as he answers it and walks out of the room without sparing me a second glance.

Did we just have a moment? I don't know. Was it loaded? Oh yes, it was. My chest still rise and fell with rapid breaths as I try to get my bearings. For the first time since I met Steven, I wonder if he liked me too. Was Emma right? Was this arrangement a stepping stone to change the dynamics between us?

***

"You've been distracted all day. What's the matter?" Emma asks, her gaze concerned as she searches my face. I shake my head and look away from her, not knowing how to respond to her comment.

"Nothing. I'm not distracted. Just worried about the show tomorrow," I answer. Lenny sits beside Emma, and I can feel both of them staring at me with suspicion in their eyes. I know I'm acting weird, but how can I not, when the guy I've liked for the past three years showed interest in me, for the first time, last night?

"You'll do great. I'm sure of it," Emma pats

me on the shoulder, reaching across the table. I force a smile on my face and nod. I'm not all that worried about the show now because our last practices have been amazing. We've been nailing it, and I have confidence that we'll do well despite being a little nervous. The problem is not the show; it's the man I've come to live in the same house with.

I don't answer, getting back to my food quietly. I'm scared that if I open my mouth, I'll tell my friends all about my conversation with Steven last night and go on to dissect it once again like I've been doing it mentally, every couple of hours, since last night.

I know better than to read too much into a simple conversation, especially when Steven and I barely talk at the uni. He is distant and almost refuses to recognize me at times, especially when he is with his friends. I'm pretty sure his aloofness has something to do with his friends and his confession during breakfast the other day.

I want to ask him what he meant by what he said, but yet again, I don't want to get my hopes too high and assume things that aren't there. I don't want him to think that I like him, even though I do, and have been thinking about him constantly, even though I have.

"You are acting weird, Maddy. I think there is a story there," Lenny points out, and I want to slap him. Moron.

"I am not acting weird, and there is nothing to tell. I doubt Emma wouldn't know if something exciting or equally tragic happened in my life," I reply, cutting him a glare. He raises his hands as if in surrender and smiles.

"All right. All right. You are not hiding

anything from us. I didn't mean to piss you off," he replies.

"I am not pissed off. I just don't appreciate being doubted," I sigh, lowering my head into my hands. Emma watches me silently, and I know she is making her own theories in her head. I hope they are nothing too crazy. Who am I kidding? Knowing my best friend, I know she will come up with the most bizarre theory.

When we are done with lunch, Lenny leaves us, to go to a band meeting. I walk out of the cafeteria with Emma, a coffee in hand. I am quiet, unusually so, and I can see why Emma is concerned, but I don't know how to tell her or rather what to tell her.

"I am not going to push you, Maddy. But if you want to talk about what has you looking so lost in thought, I am here for you," Emma's hand slips into my unoccupied one, and she squeezes.

"Nothing is troubling me. Really," I tell her. "I am just very confused. I will tell you what is going on once I figure out myself about what the hell is going on." I give her a small smile.

Emma nods in understanding, her face grim but open. She tugs on my hand as she pulls me toward the university building. "Let's get to class then. And I expect a line-by-line narration of what happened, after you figure it out," she says, and I let out a short laugh.

I expect to give her nothing less than a line-by-line narration. Whenever I decide to tell Emma about the conversation, the… moment, I will give her every little detail. I enter the building and instantly spot Steven standing by the lockers with his friends. I look at him, my gaze automatically finding him. He glances at me briefly before turning back to his friends, no recognition or friendliness in his face, like it is when we are alone at the house.

There is no indication that he had cornered me, had asked me who the man was who took my virginity, as though he would find him and hold him accountable for it. This is why I am so confused. I can't deal with the double-facedness. It makes my head reel.

***

CHAPTER EIGHTEEN

Steven Jones

The college campus is buzzing with activity. The sun has set, and the whole campus has been set up with colored lights and beautiful decorations. I look around in awe as I walk through the crowd. The theater at the back of the campus is the main center of attraction tonight. Tonight, 'A Midsummer's Night Dream' is being performed in the university theater, starring Madeline Scott.

I am dressed in a casual flannel shirt and jeans, a cap covering my face. The students don't pay me a second glance as I weave my way through the crowd. Thankfully, tonight my friends didn't make any plans for us. I didn't want to miss the show.

The excitement of people as they filter through the parking lot into the campus and make their way to the theater reaches me, and I smile. Madeline deserves to be seen. She deserves to be famous, to be as popular as any other star out there. She is not a wannabe like Gia said. She is an actor, through and through.

I slip into the theater with a cold can of coke in my hand, slipping into the corner seat. The seats are mostly empty since there are still twenty minutes for the show to start. I came early because I didn't want to get in at rush time or risk being texted or called by a friend. Actually, I have left my phone at home, so the others can't annoy me right now.

Tonight, I want to be the Steven whom Madeline sees around the house on a daily basis. I plan on catching her after the show and congratulating her. I don't want to be a shadow in her life anymore.

The other night, I wanted to tell her that I want to bring her mother's fears to life. I wanted to let her know that I am interested in her, as more than just a housemate. I want to be a permanent presence in her life. But I couldn't. I don't think I have the balls to let her have a place in my life. The others will come for me, if I do. And if I did, I will no longer hold the respect that I have right now.

I shake my head, discarding the thoughts as I settle deeper into my seat, pulling my cap over my face. A group of people enter the theater, their cackles echoing off the walls. I recognize the voice of one of them immediately.

"Let's see what all the fuss is about," Gia sneers as she walks down the ramp, followed by my entire friend group. I frown as I watch them take seats a few rows down from mine. I don't know what they are doing here. I have never seen them here before.

The worst part is that they didn't call me or tell me that they were about to come to the theater. The only other friend missing from the group is Logan. Is he not invited either? Or is he just late?

I want to walk up to my friends and ask them what this fuss is about. I want to know what they are doing here. But I am scared all of a sudden. For Madeline. I don't know why, but my stomach sours and I want to throw up.

The curtains open as the audience settle into

their seats. The show is sold out, I realize with a burst of pride. The poster of the play, spread all over campus and even in the city, seems to be doing its job. The official page of our university also did an extensive promotion for the play, for the past few weeks, and the hard work seems to have paid off.

I can still feel the discomfort in my gut at the presence of my friends, but I push it aside as the play begins. The audience quiets, my group being the last one, cracking a few insulting jokes before the people around them ask them to 'shush'. I am glad that there are others who are willing to stand up to the jerks.

I feel my cheeks heat with embarrassment and shame even though I am not sitting with them, I am still one of them. I wonder when other people look at me, they see that I'm just like Gia, Nick, Layla, and the others from my group. I wonder if

I am perceived as a stuck-up rich brat too. I hope not.

I shake the thoughts from my head when the first scene begins, or rather, the thoughts fly right out of my head. I get comfortable, taking a sip of my coke as I turn my attention to the stage, rather than the storm that has kicked up inside me.

***

The play is a huge success. The audience goes wild at the end when all the characters walk on stage, bowing at the crowd with smiles on their faces. I am happy to see that the actors got the exposure they deserve, but I am the happiest for Madeline, who is standing in the middle. She is the one who takes the microphone and steps forward, addressing the crowd in the end.

Her speech is short and simple. She tells the audience that she is grateful that they gave the play a chance and that they were here to support her friends and her.

She goes on to thank the faculty for helping them with the props, the special effects, and their time and patience. She is a sight to behold with her charming smile and her beautiful, beautiful dress.

As her speech comes to an end, the crowd cheers once more, a few people getting to their feet as they clap. But through the cheers and applause comes a voice, and I tense in my seat.

"You wannabe actors will never get anywhere in life. These shitty-ass plays aren't going to get you the fame you so desperately want. Especially you, Madeline. I know for a fact that the only way you will ever get a chance on the big screen is if you whore yourself out to the director or producer of the film." A woman's voice, muffled by a piece of clothing, echoes through the theater.

My gaze drifts to the row in front of me where my friends are sitting. Gia is missing from her seat, and I feel my stomach hollowing out as I realize that maybe this was her idea of revenge.

The theater goes silent. Madeline stands in the center of the stage, her hands still wrapped tightly around the microphone. I want to get up from my seat and walk to the stage. I want to put my hands over her ears and shield her from the way people are whispering in the seats around me.

Idiots. All of them are idiots. The applause and cheers have come to a halt, and everyone is staring at the stage as if waiting for the woman to react. Madeline says nothing. She just stands there frozen for a moment before she turns and walks out of the stage, her gait sure and silent.

Once she leaves, the curtains drop. The murmurs in the crowd grow, and my friends begin to laugh once more. I stay seated as they get up from their seats and walk out of the theater, not bothering to lower their voices as they pass nasty comments about Madeline that has me clenching my fists to keep myself from doing something I will regret.

I walk out of my own seat and excusing myself to the rushing crowd, needing to get to Madeline as quickly as I can. I want to make sure that she is alright. I mean, of course she is not okay. After what happened right now, I doubt that anyone would be okay. I pull my cap lower on my face, looking around to see if my friends are still hanging around. I see the group walking toward the parking lot, with Gia at the front.

I clench my jaw, refraining from running up to her and punching her, flat across her face. I know a man shouldn't hit a woman, but the urge is so strong at the moment that I can barely think of a reason why I should spare her.

I hurry my steps as I round the theater and walk to the back of the building, in search of the back entrance. I find it almost immediately, slipping inside and looking around for the changing rooms. I see the changing rooms in a far corner. I walk up to them, dodging the other actors.

They don't seem to pay any attention to me, talking among themselves about what just happened. I want to ask them to shut up, to stop talking so Madeline doesn't have to relive the moment, but I can't shut their mouths, can I?

I find Madeline's room that had her name on, and crack open the door to find her inside. I knock lightly and see her form tense.

She is sitting with her back turned to me, and

I can't see the look on her face, but I can almost feel the hopelessness radiating from her.

"Maddy," I called her name, and she turned around immediately, her eyes going wide. "May I come in?" I asked, watching as her gaze lowered to the floor. She is not crying. Her eyes are dry, and she looks composed enough, and I hope that is a good thing. For some reason, the thought brings me little relief.

Slowly, she nods, and I walk inside, closing the door after me. I walk up to her and sit down beside her on the small bench, in the middle of the room where she is sitting. I glance at her sideways, wondering how to ask her about how she is doing.

"She really went for the kill, huh?" Madeline asks, letting out a mirthless laugh. She looks at me with bitterness in her expression that has me wincing. "So, how long did it take for you guys to plan this revenge?" She raises her eyebrows, and I realize, to my horror, that she thinks that I was involved in the stunt Gia pulled.

"You don't really believe I knew about Gia's stunt, do you?" I ask her, hoping she will respond in the negative. After the past few days of enjoying each other's company, becoming friends, sharing small pieces of our past and present with each other, I thought that maybe she will start seeing me a little differently. I can't seem to believe, how wrong I was.

"I don't know what I believe in anymore, Steve." She sighs, and her voice turns a shade weaker. "I don't know why Gia is doing this. I don't know how your friends allow her to treat other people like shit. I don't know why she hates me. And I don't know what to make of this little insulting stunt that she pulled." She adds, her expression cracking slightly.

"I don't know what she was up to, I swear. She treats everyone the same, like shit. Yes, she is a little harsher on you, but I don't know why." I reply truthfully. I am not really offended that Madeline assumed that I was involved in Gia's plan. I am a little upset, yes, but not offended because I have never given her a reason to believe otherwise.

"Tonight was supposed to be about me." Madeline sniffles, looking away from me as she blinks rapidly. "I was supposed to come off as talented, special, a good actor tonight, but Gia had to ruin it. She had to turn this very important event for me, that I have been waiting for weeks, into a nightmare, a bad memory." She seethes as she gets up from her seat.

"She is a bad person, Maddy. You had nothing to do with her going psycho." I console her, but she shakes her head.

"I am not concerned about Gia not being a bad person. I am concerned about her flaws getting in my way of life." She sighs heavily, her shoulders slumping. Gia deserves to rot in hell, this is the only thought that repeats itself over and over in my head.

***

CHAPTER NINETEEN

Madeline Scott

It is quite crazy, how a night can go from being the best night of your life to being a nightmare that you can't escape. It is exactly how I feel right now. Steven and I left the changing room a few hours ago, and now he is aimlessly driving around and for what reason, I don't really know.

I have half a mind to ask him to stop loafing around and get me to the house so that I can sleep off my humiliation. Gia crossed a line tonight. No, she crossed several lines tonight, major ones at that. Where she found the audacity to humiliate and embarrass me in public is beyond me. And the worst part is that no one will hold her accountable.

She hid herself before speaking, and her voice was muffled, but if one knew her closely like I do, they would recognize her immediately. Like I did. Like Steven did. And like the rest of the cast did. I couldn't look at my fellow actors in the eye, as I escaped through the back door of the theater, with Steven in tow.

They didn't try to stop me either. They didn't offer their apologies or tell me that it was alright and that Gia was just being a bitch. They just stood there, whispering to each another, and that is what got to me the most. I spent the last two years as the captain of the drama club and I did my best to make each one of the actors comfortable, confident, and even daring. But when I really needed their support tonight, they were nowhere to be found.

"Enough," I say out loud as I fist my hands in my lap. Steven glances at me briefly before looking at the road again.

"What do you mean?" He asks, and I shake my head. Enough is enough. I am done being the clown. I am done standing up for people who won't stand up for me. Or themselves for that matter.

"I am quitting the drama club," I say, my voice ringing with finality. I don't want to do this anymore. I need some time away. I need to stop.

"You can't do that!" Steven exclaims, hitting the brakes. I lurch forward in my seat, grabbing onto my seatbelt. I look at him with a questionable look in my eyes.

"I can and I am," I tell him. I can very well quit acting altogether. I don't think anyone would want me, after Gia's stunt tonight. Moreover, there were supposed to be important people in the crowd. I had heard a rumor that an acting agency was sending a scout to take a look at the play. I can't show my face there again, after what Gia did. I don't want to be humiliated like that, ever again.

Every human being has a breaking point. A point after which the pain gets too much, the humiliation gets too loud. This is mine.

"You were amazing on stage tonight, Maddy. You can't just give up, because you are so talented, so capable. You were born to be an actor. You can't just stop now," Steven kills the engine and turns to face me fully.

I give him a small smile, grateful for his words, but they are not enough to lessen the pain I feel. I felt like an outsider among my own people today all because I dared to do something Gia didn't want me to do.

"You see one show and you decide I shouldn't quit. I have been acting my whole life, Steve. I have thought my decision through. And I am really glad you came to see me tonight, but I don't think you will ever see me on stage. Not for now at least," I answer.

I know that am not ready to give up on my dream altogether, but I want to take some time away.

I don't know if the time that I need is days or years, but I need to be away from these people who call themselves my co-stars, these people for whom I worked day and night to make them feel at home, make them feel like a star.

"Who told you that that this was the first time I came to watch you?" Steven asks, making me frown. I have never seen him at a show before. I doubt I would have seen him today if he hadn't come to my changing room to check up on me. The butterflies that take flight in my stomach at the thought are a crazy bunch.

"What do you mean?" I raise my eyebrows.

"I have seen every play you have ever done since freshman year, Maddy. I have been there for every show, big or small," he replies, an emotion I can't quite put a finger on entering his eyes and crowding his expression.

I blink at him, trying to make sense of his words. I know what he means, but I am trying to think of every possible meaning so that I don't make a fool of myself. Is he saying what I think he is?

"You're lying," I accuse him, my voice sounding breathless for some reason. The humiliation of tonight, the sadness and betrayal, all disappear as Steven shakes his head, reaching forward and taking my hand in his.

"I am not. I can swear on everything I love that I have been there for all your plays. From Macbeth to Volpone to Julius Caesar, I have seen every one of them," he says as he squeezes my hand for emphasis, and a tingle shoots up my arm.

"There is no way," I shake my head, refusing to believe what he is saying. "How come no one saw you then? How come the others at the university still believe that you will never be interested in drama because it's lame?" I ask, cocking an eyebrow at him.

"I am not interested in drama, Maddy," he shrugs. "But to answer your question, I come in full disguise so no one ever recognizes me. I have a reputation to maintain, after all."

"So why do you risk everything, just to watch my plays, especially since you don't want to be recognized?" I frown, chewing on my bottom lip. This is madness. Why would I go to an event that doesn't concern me or interest me in the least bit?

"To see you," he responds. My heart skips a beat at his words because there's no way in hell that he said what he just did.

"To see me?" I ask dumbly. He nods his head in response, and I swallow, looking down at my hand, which is still in his. "Why?"

"I think you are smart enough to figure it out yourself," he answers. I want to tell him that I am not smart at all and if he wants me to know something, he will have to spell it out for me. I want to ask him if he is serious and if this is one of his pranks because if it is, I will kill him. But instead, I stay quiet.

I try to open my mouth and force something out but I can't. The words are stuck in my throat.

"I am going to let you think about what I just said. I am going to let you figure out what I am trying to tell you, on your own. You have a day. And then you can come to me and tell me if you figured it out and tell me what you think about it," Steven says as he pulls his hand out of mine gently.

I want to grab onto it and not let it go again, but I do, albeit reluctantly. "And I also want you to reconsider your decision about quitting the drama club. If you quit, Gia will get what she wants. Don't let her win, Maddy."

His words stay with me as he starts the engine and begins driving again. After an hour or so, he pulls up in front of the house. I get out of the car and walk to the front door, unlocking it and slipping inside quietly. My head is a tumult of thoughts, and my heart's a mess. I don't know what to think, what to assume. Not right now, at least. So I decide to sleep and think about it later. Calling a good night over my shoulder, I walk up to my room and slip into bed, pulling the covers over me. I don't bother to change tonight.

***

Emma sits across from me on her bed, her lips pursed and eyes wide, as if she is holding back her words, ready to burst out. Gianna is not in the room; she went out to meet her boyfriend. I chose this time to come over, precisely to avoid her, as I'm sure I don't want her overhearing my conversation and later have her tell her friends about it.

Now that I have comfortably spilled the tea to my best friend, I wait for her response and advice. I need to know what to do. I have no idea what my life has become.

"You can speak now," I tell Emma, knowing well enough that she is waiting for me to give her a thumbs-up to blurt out everything that she is holding in.

"He totally likes you!" She squeals as she throws herself at me. I catch her in my arms, struggling to keep my balance as she hugs me. "Oh my god, he likes you!"

I let her squeal some more before pulling away from her, a nervous expression on my face. "Are you sure that is what he was trying to tell me?" I ask.

"He told you that he is interested in you. What

more do you need, darling?" She raises her eyebrows, eyeing me warily. I don't like the look directed toward me.

"I don't know, Em. What if he is just messing with my head? What if he is just trying to get in my pants?" Horror churns in my gut because I didn't think about the possibility before. Shit. Shit. Shit.

"Maddy, baby, calm down. You are overthinking it, alright? Steven told you that he likes you. He confessed about going to the theater shows every year to see you, and he came to console you when you were sad. I am so sorry, I couldn't be the one by your side. Oh, how I wish I could be there for you," Emma says, her expression turning sad.

She hadn't been able to come to my show last night because her mother needed her at home. Emma lives in California but chooses to live at the dorm to escape a very toxic family environment.

"It's not your fault. Don't be sorry. I know you are here for me now, and that is what matters to me," I say, taking her hand in mine and squeezing. "Also, I can't bring myself to believe that Steven is showing genuine interest in me. I still think it's a game though," I frown.

"No, no. Why would you think like that?" Emma asks.

"I don't know, Em. He doesn't talk to me when he is around his friends. He doesn't even acknowledge my existence in university. Only when we are alone within the four walls of the house, does he make a move to talk to me, speak to me as a friend.

"You know how his friends are, Maddy. I think he is just trying to save you from Gia's wrath.

I doubt she will leave you alone if she ever finds out that Steven likes you," she points out.

I nod my head as I consider her words. I didn't think about it that way. I sigh as I tuck my hair behind my ear, closing my eyes and finally making up my mind. I will talk to Steven tonight, for my sake.

Emma is right. Maybe I should just go for the kill. If he doesn't feel the same way, so be it. I am holding onto a little hope, and it will be enough to see me through this night.

***

CHAPTER TWENTY

Steven Jones

Logan and I walk down the hallway to our next class. It is one of the two classes that I share with him, and I am really glad. He is the only tolerable friend of mine, and I enjoy spending time with him, mostly because he is not rude or mean or demeaning in any way.

"Did you hear about what happened last night

at the theater?" He asks me as we enter the class and take our usual seats in the back. I pretend to frown and be oblivious to what he is talking about. I told my friends that I was at home last night, finishing up the remainder of my assignments, and that my phone died, so I have no idea what went down at the show.

"What happened? The others were talking about it too, at lunch time, but I didn't catch much." I shrug indifferently as I pull out my notebook and pen from my bag and put them on the table in front of me.

"Gia insulted Maddy at the sold-out show," Logan informs me. Despite having witnessed everything firsthand, I feel my jaw clenching at the information, at the reminder of how low Gia could stoop.

"The others can't stop talking about it.

Apparently, after the way Maddy insulted her at the party, Gia started to plan her revenge. And yesterday, she finally put her plan into action. She paid off the others in charge of lighting and the sound system to use the microphone at the end, after the captain has given her speech."

I feel my teeth ache from how hard I am gritting them together, but I can't bring myself to care. Gia has gone too low this time. I don't think I will ever be able to be civil with her after what she did last night.

"Gia is fucking crazy," Logan adds, making me glance at him. His expression has darkened, and I wonder if I am not the only one who thinks of her behavior as disrespectful and her attitude as insufferable. "Ruining someone's night, that too a big night for Maddy from what I have heard, is not acceptable at all." He shakes his head, turning to his book.

I feel the urge to tell Logan then that I think the same, that I have been wanting to say the same since I saw her getting into it with Maddy the first time, but I keep my mouth shut. The professor walks into the class, and I feel myself relaxing. I don't want to push my luck. If Logan is someone like me, who is only with the group for the popularity but doesn't really think what they do is right, then I have truly found myself a good friend.

But I don't want to hurry into this new, stronger bond I feel with Logan. I am going to let it grow, let it nurture. I like this guy, I decide. I have never heard one of my other group members talking about Madeline like he did, with an expectation and surety that I think about it constantly. I am glad that I am not the only one who sees her potential. She needs supporters in her life.

"How is she doing, by the way? After the stunt

Gia pulled?" Logan whispers to me, pulling me out of my thoughts.

"I don't know. I don't really talk to her. We live in the same house, Lo. But we are not best friends." I chuckle nervously. Last night, I told her how I feel about her, how I see her. Maybe it is the reason why I feel so nervous all of a sudden or maybe I feel as if I will get caught if I say anything that I am not supposed to share with anyone else.

"You should check up on her. I heard she was amazing last night, before the whole fiasco with Gia. Let her know that, maybe." Logan pats me on the shoulder, and I nod, turning to my notebook.

My throat feels tight, and I feel my chest expand. I really need someone who gets how much I like Madeline, how much I want her. But I still keep my mouth shut. I don't want to spill too much too soon. One step at a time, I tell myself as

I focus on the lecture. One step at a time.

***

I come back home after practice to find the whole house smelling of garlic and seasoning and… pasta. I don't know how I pinpoint the exact dish that is being prepared in the kitchen, but I just know. I grin as I make my way into the kitchen to find Madeline in front of the stove, dressed in comfy pajamas with her apron on.

Music flows through the kitchen as she cooks, swaying her hips a little to the beat. I watch her for a moment, wanting to freeze this moment in time. After last night, I was scared that she would retreat into a shell, and that I won't see her laughing and smiling like she does. I have never been this glad to be wrong.

"What are you making?" I ask as I compose myself, walking deeper into the kitchen. She turns to face me, a smile lighting up her face at the sight of me. I return it as she gestures at the pasta that I have come to fall in love with.

"Pasta. My mom's recipe. Remember?" She asks me, as if I can ever forget something that is remotely even related to her life.

"I see," I say as I lean against the counter and watch her. Logan's words come back to me in the moment, so I ask, "How are you holding up, Mads?" The nickname rolls off my tongue easily as if I have been calling her that my whole life. I like how it sounds on my tongue.

Madeline pauses as if realizing that I didn't call her Maddy or Madeline, but she doesn't comment on it. She just shrugs, tossing the pasta into the pan of sauce. "I am doing okay, I guess. I went to the drama club meeting today regardless of my decision to quit. I blame you." She throws me a look, but my smile just grows.

"I am glad you decided to go." I step closer to her. She puts the lid on the pasta after adding the cheese and turns to look up at me. "You deserve to be seen." I add, leaning forward and kissing the top of her head before I can think too much of it.

Madeline's shoulders tense, and her expression freezes. I wonder if I have offended her as she looks up at me, unblinking. I would have laughed at her reaction if I wasn't so nervous about crossing a line and pushing her away. I am not trying to scare her off. I want to get closer to her, not farther away from her.

"I-I'm sorry," I begin because maybe I should apologize and make it better before it gets worse, but Madeline cuts me off.

"You like me?" She asks, catching me off-guard. It is my turn to blink at her in shock and nerves now. I clear my throat before speaking again.

"Yes, I do." I answer. "Took you long enough to figure it out." I give her a rueful smile. Her eyes narrow at me, and she steps forward, smacking me on my upper arm.

"You couldn't have said it last night?" She asks. "I have been fretting my ass off all day wondering if I read it wrong, if you didn't mean what I thought you meant." She adds.

"Lady, I thought it was obvious that I liked you when I didn't stop bringing you, bunch of afternoon coffees, even after you already decided to move into my house." I point out. The fact that she hasn't told me to fuck off yet or told me that she is moving out or that she can't stand to see my face gives me some hope. I cling to it desperately.

Madeline's expression turns thoughtful for a moment before she says, "Yes, you did. But you never acknowledge me at university, when you are around your friends. What am I supposed to do with these mixed signals?" She raises her eyebrows questioningly.

I feel my cheeks heat at the fact that she noticed me not acknowledging her in university. But I have a solid reason for that. "My friends don't particularly like you, and I don't want them troubling you more than you already are." I explain.

"Emma said the same thing." She nods.

"Emma knows?" I ask, a pang of fear entering my heart. If she happens to tell anyone, it's over for me. My friends will kill Madeline and then me.

"Of course, she does," Madeline says before

she looks at my face. "Is that a problem?" She asks, a frown settling between her brows.

"I don't want people to find out, Mads. They will make the rest of the year hell for the both of us." I sigh, running a hand through my hair.

"Emma isn't going to make our lives hell. She has been rooting for you and me, ever since day one. And she won't tell anyone else either." Madeline's hand reaches for mine, and she takes it in hers. Squeezing once, she smiles at me. "I understand that we can't be together in public, Steve. I get it that the others won't let us. I won't blame you for trying to keep your feelings for me a secret. God knows I have, too." She assures me.

I feel my heart filling to the brim at her words. "So, is this you confessing to me, Madeline Scott?" I ask, feeling a grin so huge tugging on my lips that my cheeks hurt.

Madeline looks away from me, her eyes widening. I follow her gaze to find the pasta still simmering on the stove. Gasping a little, she pulls her hand out of mine and turns the stove off, sighing softly as she straightens.

"I almost burned it," she breathes out.

"You never answered my question," I tell her. She glances at me, and a pink tint takes over her cheeks.

"If you want to hear it, then yes, I like you," she admits, and I let out a soft grunt as I pull her toward me. I wrap my arms around her, burying my face in her neck because, hell, I've been waiting for this moment for the past three years.

"You just made me the happiest man alive," I tell her, mumbling into her ear.

"I doubt that," she chuckles. I pull away from her, my expression turning serious. I want her to know how much control and power she have over me, has had over me for the past three years.

"I've liked you ever since I saw you around campus with your friends, laughing and chatting and living life like I'd never seen anyone live, Mads. I've been holding myself back, for all these years because I knew you don't like jocks. I guess, I was scared to make a fool of myself in front of you. So, when I say you've made me the happiest man right now, I mean it," I confess, looking her in the eye with every ounce of sincerity that I own.

"You're crazy," she shakes her head. Her voice wavers slightly, and I pull her against my chest once more, kissing the top of her head.

"I blame you because you're the only one who makes me feel this crazy, and for whom I'm okay being this crazy," I tell her, and she giggles against my chest, wrapping her arms around me. And for the first time since I moved in, my house feels like home to me.

***

CHAPTER TWENTY-ONE

Madeline Scott

I have no idea what the hell just happened, but I know that after Steven and I pull apart, we go into the dining room to have our dinner. My celebratory pasta is a success because we agree to be together, be exclusive... but in secret.

I know it might seem like a red flag to many, for us to keep our relationship a secret, but I think it is the best that we can do right now. University ends in six months. Then we can be dating in public or whatever because then, we will not be part of this community and can live our life on our terms.

We can live our lives however we want it, because who we date is our business, but after the stunt Gia pulled on the night of the show, I don't want to take any risks. I got weird looks and murmurs all morning when I walked into class, and I don't want a repeat of it. I am sure that Gia will do way worse if she finds out that I am dating Steven.

Once we were done with dinner, Steven leaves the dining room to call his parents because his father has been troubling him again. I go to my room to call Emma and tell her about the new development. I asked Steven if it was okay if I told my best friend, and he agreed as long as Emma doesn't tell anyone else.

I dial my best friend and walk over to my bed, lowering myself onto it. I can't contain my excitement because the past two hours doesn't seem real but all too real at the same time. I want to squeal and dance around my room. I want to wrap my arms around Steven and not let go. I don't know how I managed to let go of him in the kitchen.

He seems to be as whipped as I am because he didn't want to leave me alone either. He kept delaying the call until the clock struck ten, and he realized that maybe calling his father and then spending time with me would be a much better idea.

Emma picks up her phone on the third ring, her voice bored. "Hello, Maddy," she says, and I hear her yawn. I can bet a thousand dollars that she is studying right at this moment.

"Are you studying right now?" I ask, glancing at the wall clock in my room. It shows that it is already ten-fifteen. What else is she doing up so late, other than studying?

"Yes, I am. I am trying to study for a class test tomorrow. Anyway, why'd you call? Is everything alright?" She asks, making me roll my eyes. She makes it seem like I call her only when I need something from her or something is going wrong in my life.

"Steven and I are together," I answer, not wanting to wait any longer to get the news to her. There is a pause on the other end of the line, and I wonder if she has hung up the call.

"Come again?" She asks. I have to swallow my giggles and squeals as I speak once more, repeating what I said before. But then I add, "Don't make a sound. Don't repeat it after me. It's a secret. I told you because you are my best friend. No one else in university should know about it, alright?"

"What? Why?" Emma asks, her voice high-pitched, telling me that she was about to squeal and shout the words out at the top of her lungs.

"Because I don't want any more complications in my life, Em. I have gotten what I wanted for three years now, and I am not going to ruin it. I think it is best if we keep our relationship a secret," I explain to her exactly why we are not going public until the end of the college year.

"Wow. Okay," my best friend breathes. I bite my lip and wait for her to say more. "God, Maddy, it feels surreal," she adds.

"I know. I have been pining over him for so

many years, Em. And apparently, he has been, too. It is not a prank, not a joke. It is a hundred percent real," I tell her. I am bursting with excitement. I never thought I could get Steven. Even in my dreams, I am the one running after him. Never before did I consider that he might be running after me, too.

"Can I meet him at least?" She asks. "I need to put the bestie approval stamp on him." I chuckle and tell her that we can meet somewhere outside of uni.

"I will talk to him and let you know," I say. This time, she lets out a small squeal, shutting up only a moment later.

"Alright then. Gianna is up and snapping at me for being too loud. I will meet you tomorrow, and I want to know everything, line-by-line narration, remember?" She asks, and I nod my head before remembering that she cannot see me through the phone.

"Yes, ma'am," I say. We say our goodbyes, and I hang up the phone, place it on my nightstand and lay back down on my bed. I stare up at the ceiling, still feeling the high from a few hours ago. I am in a relationship. After years of avoiding being in one, ever since my ex cheated on me, I am going to be in a relationship and that too, with the man I have liked since the moment I saw him on the soccer field.

I smile to myself, clutching a pillow to my chest as I press my cheek against it. Steven is mine. Even if to the world, we are incompatible, in this house, in our hearts, we are irrevocably and completely each other's.

***

Emma stares at Steven, who is sitting beside

me in the booth across from ours. It's been three days since we started dating, and today, he decided to meet my best friend and get the stamp of approval. Steven is dressed for the occasion, looking extremely handsome in a plain white shirt and a pair of blue jeans. A silver chain hangs from his neck, and he fidgets with it from time to time.

Emma's gaze drops to his hand as it comes up to touch the eagle pendant again, and I slap his hand away. He gives me a sheepish look, and I glare at him. What is he doing? He is not this nervous all the time.

"So, I realize that you are dating my best friend," Emma finally speaks up. The waiter had taken our orders a few minutes ago, and I knew the questioning would follow soon after.

I was right because my best friend looks ready to pounce and leave Steven in pieces. I feel bad for him.

"Yes, I like Mads. Very much. I have for a very long time. It just took me a lot of time to gather the courage to tell her how I felt," he answers, his fingers interlacing with mine under the table. I feel my cheeks turn pink and my heart jump with joy in my chest at the gesture.

Emma clears her throat, making us look at her. Her stern gaze comes to rest on Steven once more. "It has also come to my attention that you want to keep your relationship a secret. Why is that? Do you care to explain, Jones?" She asks, her voice firm.

"Em, I think we talked about it—" I begin, but she shuts me up with a glare.

"It's fine, Mads. I can explain." Steven pats my hands interlaced with his as he looks at my best friend once again, a smile on his face. He doesn't look nervous anymore. "We have mutually agreed to keep our relationship a secret because we don't want third parties to try and break us apart, which is inevitable after recent events. Maddy and my friends are not on good terms, and I think other students will trouble her too if they find out that we are dating. So, it is best for us if we keep our relationship under wraps for the moment. We will announce it to the public at the end of the college year."

"That's reasonable." Emma nods her head, her lips pressing into a thin line. "I just want to make sure that the secrecy is not because you have side chicks or a woman who is pregnant with your baby and you don't want the women to know about each other." She raises her eyebrows, and Steven looks like he is about to pass out.

"I can assure you, Mads is it for me. I don't

need or want any other woman in my life—" He begins to explain himself, but Emma waves him off, grinning like the little bastard she is.

"I was just pulling your leg, Jones. I know you like my best friend. I see the way you look at her." Her expression softens as her gaze flickers over to me. "I love this! I know I can't tell Lenny now, but after the end of the year, I expect us to go on double dates," she adds excitedly.

I blush a little, wondering how my best friend can be so sure of our relationships, but Steven says, "Of course, we are going on double dates. That is the best part of having best friends." He winks at Emma, whose grin widens, taking up her entire face.

"You shouldn't put ideas into her head," I mutter to my boyfriend, who chuckles a little.

Emma's eyes narrow on me, and she hisses, "You know you like the idea too. You are just too cool to admit it."

I shake my head as a smile makes its way onto my face. I don't think I can ever say no to what she says. I know I will go on double dates with her if she insists and drag Steven along too.

Our orders arrive then, and we chat as we eat our meals. The evening proceeds smoothly. We laugh at the jokes we crack, share stories from a time when my crush on Steven was at its peak, although I would have preferred if Emma didn't tell him all the details, and then went on to make plans for the future.

I feel so at ease and comforted with by Steven by my side, probably because I have grown so used to his presence, living in the same house as him. Moreover, we have a connection, a liking for each other that I have not felt for anyone else. I am not one to compare my current love interests to my exes, so I am willing to give Steven a chance, willing to accept him with no doubts.

Emma seems happy for me. She keeps passing me soft smiles, which I know are meant to comfort me, but I don't tell her that I am feeling the most comfortable I ever have, sitting in a booth, laughing and talking and eating with my boyfriend and my best friend. I am happy and grateful for this moment, and I want to cherish it forever – the first meeting.

When we are in the car after dinner, Steven turns to me, a grin playing on his lips. "Emma is a vibe," he says, and I nod my head in agreement.

"I agree. She is my favorite person ever," I answer.

"I thought I was your favorite person," Steven frowns, making me chuckle.

"You are my favorite person romantically. Emma is my favorite person platonically," I clarify.

"I'll take that," he sighs, reaching over the center console and placing a peck on my cheek. I melt at the gesture, feeling my heart expand with warmth and gratitude once more.

***

CHAPTER TWENTY-TWO

Steven Jones

It is harder than I thought, to stay away from Maddy in university. Every time I see her, I want to walk up to her, hug her, and kiss her in front of all the students, letting them know that she is mine, that she holds my heart in her hands.

I keep stealing glances at her whenever we happen to be in the same room, and I have to remind myself that it is for our own good that we are dating in secret. I look at Gia and her obnoxious way of speaking and laughing, trying to be the center of attention, and I feel myself relaxing a little. Maddy is safe, I tell myself. As long as she is mine in secret, she is safe.

"I bought this dress on Saturday. Isn't it flattering?" Gia asks us as she approaches our table. She twirls a little, and all the guys except for Logan, Jared, and me cheer her on, whistling and hitting on her. She glances at me, and I promptly look away, turning my attention to the sandwich I am having for lunch. "What do you think, Steven?" She asks, walking up to me and perching on the edge of the table.

She crosses her legs together, trying to achieve something I don't see, as she bats her eyelashes at me. "Tell me. Is this dress worth the investment?" She asks.

I feel myself wanting to tell her that I don't know if she looks beautiful or pretty or if the dress is a good investment because I find one woman beautiful and that is my girlfriend.

As if I summoned her, Maddy walks into the cafeteria with Emma and her boyfriend, Lenny. Her gaze finds mine before looking at Gia, who is perched on the end of our table. I watch as she peels her gaze away and walks to a table in a corner of the cafeteria, not glancing at us again.

"Hello? Earth to Steven?" Gia says, waving a hand in front of my face. I snap my gaze back to hers before she looks over her shoulder, looking for the reason of my distracted self.

"I don't know, Gia. Ask someone else." I wave Gia off, looking at Maddy from the corner of my eye. My girlfriend finds my gaze, as if she can sense it on her, and a small smile lights up her face.

I feel relief flood through my chest, and I turn back to Gia, who looks like I kicked her puppy.

"What do you mean, ask someone else?" She rolls her eyes, her voice taking on a whiny tone. Someone needs to tell her that she is a grown woman and the baby voice is unbecoming.

"I want to know your opinion." Her hand reaches out, palm flattening against the center of my chest. I stiffen, looking around the table for someone to help me. None of the people who call me their friends come to my rescue. They seem to be enjoying themselves.

"Ask Nick. He has a better sense of fashion than I do," I say, gesturing at my friend sitting beside Gianna. He grins at Gia, drawling as he beckons to her, "Come to me. I will give a very thorough opinion, G."

I cringe internally at the way he eyes Gia, and just for a moment, I feel bad for her, but then she straightens, and an equally suggestive smile lights up her face. "Will you now?" She asks as she walks over to him. I sigh in relief when she removes her hand from my chest.

Logan, who sits beside me, pats me on the shoulder, and I offer him an uneasy smile. God, Gia makes me uncomfortable.

"I say we ditch these fellows and head to the field. I need to talk to the coach about the upcoming season," he murmurs in my ear. I am more than glad to get out of here, so I nod.

"Sure," I answer, picking up my sandwich and getting out of my seat. I glance at Maddy once more to find her gaze fixed on the plate in front of her. Her lips are pressed into a tight line, and she doesn't look very happy. My stomach sours as I wonder if it is because of me.

I peel my gaze away from her and start walking toward the door to the cafeteria, though because I don't want Logan to notice or, worse, Gia to understand what is going on between us. As we walk out into the open air, Logan turns to me, his expression neutral.

"Did you talk to Maddy?" he asks. My heart skips several beats at his question. I turn to face him, my eyes widening slightly.

"About what?" I respond, trying not to sound as flushed as I look.

"I asked you to check up on her, Steve," Logan gives me a strange look. I could have sworn that a small smile tugs at one corner of his lips, but who am I kidding? Logan never smiles. He is barely even amused until he is on the football field or drunk out of his mind.

"Yes, yes, I did. She is holding up fine," I shrug, once again trying to act nonchalant when I feel so much for her, care so much about her.

"Gia is going to get her karma for what she did," he mutters, and I agree with him. I hope she does. She deserves payback for every horrible thing she has done to Maddy. My girl didn't deserve any of it. But Gia will deserve every ounce of shame, sadness, and misery that will come along her way.

***

"Baby, I am back," I call to Maddy as I walk into the house, slinging my bag over my shoulder. Maddy doesn't answer as she usually does, making me frown. I walk into the living room to find her sitting on one of the couches, staring straight ahead.

Her face is void of all emotion, and she looks like a stone statue. I frown as I walk up to her and take a seat beside her.

"Mads? What's wrong?" I ask her. She turns to face me, a neutral expression on her face. She looks away from me again, and I feel my heartbeat kick up a notch.

"Maddy, tell me if something is bothering you. I don't like seeing you so upset," I say, cupping her cheek and turning her to face me.

"I don't like it when Gia touches you. Or talks to you for that matter," she replies, her voice clipped and cold. I knew her sour mood had something to do with the little bitch.

"I don't like it either," I answer truthfully.

"Then why do you let her do it?" she asks, her

expression crumpling and turning pained. I scoot closer to her, wrapping one arm around her. She tenses but then relaxes a little, snuggling closer to me.

"I don't. Yes, she touched me but I told her to go bother someone else. I don't like anyone else touching me who isn't you, Mads. I don't like it at all," I sigh against her hair, tightening my hold on her. "For me, it's you. Ever since we started dating three weeks ago, I have been the happiest I have been in a long, long time. I like you and only you, Mads. Remember that. Always," I add.

Maddy relaxes in my hold completely then, nuzzling her face against my neck. "You have a sweet mouth on you, you know that, Steve?" she asks, and I chuckle.

"Do you want to taste it?" I respond teasingly. She glances up at me, her expression darkening.

"You bet." Pushing away from me, she gets up, climbing onto my lap. She straddles me, cupping my face with both her hands as she brings her face closer to mine.

I wrap my hands around her waist, pulling her closer. It's been three weeks, and this is our first kiss. But I have been waiting for this moment for longer than three weeks. She tilts her head to the side as her lips capture mine. I sigh inwardly as my chest collapses at the first taste of her.

I kiss her softly, cherishing the moment, loving every moment of it, committing it to memory. I close my eyes as she deepens the kiss, her arm wrapping around my neck, pulling me closer. I trail my hand up to her face until I am cupping her cheek. As the kiss turns fervent and intense, I feel myself wanting more of her, more of us. I need it. And by that, I mean I want her in my future, every day.

I hate that I can't share this piece of my life with others. I hate that I have to keep her a secret because she is the only person who has ever made me want to shout at the top of my lungs and let everyone know that she is mine and that I am hers and hers only.

A thousand 'Gias' can't let me turn my back on Maddy. When I told Emma that she is it for me, I meant it. And I mean it now when I say that, every day I spend with her, I am a little happier. I have almost forgotten the time when I was so depressed that getting out of my room was a task, facing the world was unbearable.

She has taught me to smile again, and I am grateful to her. I will always be grateful to Maddy for teaching me how to live life again, for showing me that I am not alone.

We kiss for a long while, so that when we pull

away, we are both panting.

I grin at her, and she returns it, leaning forward to place another peck on my lips. "I will cut Gia's hands off if she touches you again," she threatens, her voice dripping with laughter but a seriousness ringing through it that I can't ignore.

"I will hand you the knife," I answer. She chuckles as she lays her head on my chest. I hold her close to me, letting her listen to my heartbeat that thunders in my chest. She draws lazy circles on my chest, and we stay like that for a long moment. I am glad that I showered after practice tonight because I don't think Maddy would be so comfortable laying her head on my chest and being so close to me otherwise.

"Steve?" She mumbles after a long moment.

"Hmm, baby?" I respond and feel her smile. I

like when I make her smile. It makes me feel special. It makes me feel worthy.

"I can't wait to tell the world about us," she answers. I nod my head.

"I can't either."

"People are stupid. I wish I could tell everyone that I have the best boyfriend in the world who knows how to play soccer and gets me coffee every afternoon so I don't get grumpy," she responds, making me chuckle.

"And I wish I could tell everyone that my girlfriend is the most amazing woman ever who is going to make it big as an actor and cooks me pasta when I have had a long day," I answer. Maddy looks up at me, her face serene and calm and happy.

"I like it when you call me an amazing actor," she grins.

"I called you an amazing girlfriend who will make it big as an actor," I correct her. Her grin dissolves, and she scowls at me.

"It's the same thing. Don't ruin the moment, Jones," she smacks me on the chest lightly. I wrap my hand around her wrist and bring it to my lips, placing a kiss on her knuckles.

"I am sorry," I say, and she smiles once more. Kissing me on the chest, she lays her head back on it as I ask her about her day. I feel fulfilled tonight like I have felt every night since Maddy walked into my life.

***

CHAPTER TWENTY-THREE

Madeline Scott

I tap my foot against the floor impatiently

as I wait for Emma to show up. I am standing at the entrance of the university, staring at the opposite end where the dorms are. My best friend is late today, and I am getting impatient. Class starts in fifteen minutes, and I can't help but feel anxious. I don't like showing up to class late; it makes me uneasy and embarrassed.

I lean against one of the statues at the front lawn of the campus, glancing at my watch, then back at the dorms, hoping I stared hard enough, she will materialize at the front gate out of thin air. I am earlier than usual today because I had the day off at the cafe. This is the first time that I have taken a day off since Steven and I were up, late last night, and I needed to rest a little.

The finals are close, and the pressure is on. Steven and I decided that it would be best if we studied together and held each other accountable. We did manage to get a lot done last night in our respective subjects, so I guess our plan worked.

I feel someone walk up to me but don't turn to look at them, still waiting for Emma to come out of the dorms and manifest in front of me with the power of my stares. But then the person opens their mouth, and I feel my heart drop to my stomach like lead.

"Hello, Madeline," Gia croons, putting her arm on my shoulder as if we are best of friends. I turn to look at her, frowning as I lower my shoulder and get out of her touch. Her arm drops dramatically, and the girl standing next to her lets out a small chuckle.

Gia turns to glare at her, and the girl quickly shuts up, straightening and hiking her bag higher over her shoulder. Once she is satisfied that she has the upper hand, she turns her attention back to me.

"How are you doing? I heard what happened at the theater on the night of the show. So tragic," she puts a hand on her heart and feigns a hurt expression as if she hadn't been the one to pull the stunt.

And the fact that it has been weeks since the night of the show, and she decides to bring it up now, when I was over the whole incident. Bitch.

"Tragic indeed how some people don't know what to do with their time but trouble others for the sake of it," I smile at her, deciding not to fall for her words. If she thinks that her little stunt is going to stop me from standing up to her, she is gravely mistaken.

"Is that so?" Gia asks, tilting her head to the side. "I heard that you were called out for who you truly are," she adds, sneering at me.

"People with no talent know nothing but to bring down the ones who do. If you think that I was offended, you're sorely mistaken. I like that I have an anti-fan club who thinks so highly of me, that they make a fool of themselves, trying to bring me down in front of others," I wave her off. Suddenly I see Emma walking through the front gates of the uni then, and I let out a breath. Finally.

"You think you are all that, no?" Gia gets into my face, making me look at her. I frown at her, wondering if she knows how cringey and cliché she sounds.

"I don't know what you mean. I don't want to know what you mean," I reply. It's true; I don't want to know what the hell she is talking about. She can go and fuck herself for all I care. I don't want to do anything with her now.

"Hey, Maddy," Emma throws her arm over my shoulder as she reaches me, turning to look at Gia and her crony who is still standing wordlessly at her side. "We are getting late for class; let's go," she adds, steering me away from the two women.

I am glad that she intervened because I was scarily close to breaking Gia's nose. I am already pissed at her for hitting on my boyfriend when he has made it clear, time and time again that he is not interested in her. I trust Steven on this one because I have seen Gia try to hit on other girls' boyfriends before. It is as if since she can't get one of her own, she goes after every man, taken or not.

"She is getting on my last nerves, and I will kill her someday," I mutter under my breath so only Emma hears it. We hurry inside the building, eager to get to class.

"And I will help you bury the body," my best friend responds, humoring me. I chuckle then, shaking my head because I know that if I ever decide to get rid of Gia once and for all, Emma will be right by my side, ready to help me. I love how accurate whomever the person was, the one who said that best friends don't let you do stupid things as long as you do it with them.

***

I sit in my chair at the head of the table in the

drama club. The other students are sitting around me, staring at me and waiting for me to speak. I look down at my phone, scrolling through the comments on our show, the one which ended in a disaster. It was not the night of my dreams, but the comments we have received were straight out of my dreams.

I let a smile make its way onto my face as I turn to my co-actors. I see their faces light up with hope too, at the look on mine. This is why I believe in smiling all the time, especially at strangers. You are going to make their day, trust me, until they aren't a bitch who never learned how to smile growing up.

After what happened that night, I was a little nervous coming to the first drama club meeting, but when I did, the others immediately walked up to me and offered me words of encouragement that I didn't get that day after the disaster at the show. I feel much more comfortable around my team now than I did before. I think Gia's stunt just brought us all closer, and I am glad I took Steven's advice and decided to keep acting even though I wanted to quit.

"The reviews are amazing! The video that the uni's official channel put up on YouTube has over a million views!" I announce, and cheers go around the room as my team hugs each other and congratulates me. "I am so happy for us! We deserve it. After all the work we put in, we deserve it!" I add.

"We are glad to have you as our captain, Maddy. I don't think any of us would have dared to go all out on the props, costumes, and sound effects like you did," Harry, one of our teammates, says, smiling at me.

I return his smile, thanking him for his kind

words.

My teammates are the reason why I didn't give up. After the last couple of shows, which didn't do so well, there was tension and anxiety among the members, as to how this play would go. I think we have overcome our fears now. It is also sad that this was our last major show of the year, and now we all have to get into studying for the exams and preparing for soccer season.

Although nobody knows it, I have been a good girlfriend and am going to watch Steven's practice after my classes are done. I always sit on the farthermost bleachers, pretending to be studying during the practice so no one gets suspicious of me. I love watching Steven in action.

I have attended all of his games since I started uni and met Gia there for the first time, when she saw me cheering Steven on. I have a feeling that maybe she hates me because she thinks I like Steven. I mean she wouldn't be wrong, but it doesn't sit right with me that she has been such a pain in my ass, over a guy.

When the drama club meeting comes to an end, I make my way to the bleachers once more to watch Steven play. I freeze when I get to my usual spot because a few rows over sit Gia and her group of minions along with Gianna.

I am contemplating, either to sit on the bleachers and pretend like I do every day just to watch my boyfriend to secretly cheer him on or to leave, when Gianna glances over my shoulder and spots me. She smiles at me as she gets up from her little friend group and walks over to me.

"Hey, Maddy! Long time no see. Ever since you moved out of the dorms, I haven't seen you," she says as she walks over to me. The other girls are looking at us; Gia's glare searing through my very soul, but I focus on the woman in front of me. I like Gianna. She is fun, kind, and nice, so I ignore the others and grin at her.

"I came to visit Emma a few days ago, but I missed you. I really missed you!" I say as she wraps her arms around me, pulling me into a friendly hug. I don't know if she doesn't get the shit from the other girls, for being friends with me or rather, her boyfriend's friends, but I am glad she doesn't care about them.

"I missed you, too, love. I have been asking Steven to ask you to come out with us for days now. But I get why he doesn't want you to tag along." Gianna's lips turn down in a frown as she glances over her shoulder at Gia, who is whispering to the other girls as if I don't already know that she is talking about me.

"It's okay. I would rather not come than do and regret it all night," I chuckle. "How are you and Jared doing?" I ask as we settle down on the bleachers. I glance out at the field, spotting Steven immediately. The coach has the guys lined up and is shouting orders at them that I can't quite hear.

"We are doing really well. I still have him wrapped around my little finger," Gianna says, and I look at her to find her wiggling her eyebrows at me. I let out a laugh as I pat her knee.

"Of course, you do. I love that for you," I answer, turning to look at Steven once more.

"And I hear that you have Steven wrapped around yours these days." She leans forward and whispers into my ear. I choke on my saliva and let out a cough as I glance at her.

"Whoever told you that?" I ask, my eyes

widening. Oh, hell no. If the word got out about us, we are screwed.

"Logan has been coming up with theories of you two these days," Gianna shrugs as she glances at the field, at the hulk of a man, who is Steven's best friend.

"He is tripping," I let out a nervous laugh, making a mental note to tell Steven about it. I glance at Gia, and Gianna pats me on the shoulder.

"She doesn't know. We know better than to tell her about the two of you. But if it's true, my love, I am so happy for you," Gianna lets out a high-pitched squeal, throwing her arms over my shoulder and pulling me into another hug. I don't know how I feel about this news.

***

CHAPTER TWENTY-FOUR

Steven Jones

"I didn't know you were such good friends with Madeline, Gianna," Gia says, popping a chip into her mouth and glaring at Jared's girlfriend.

She seems unbothered by the tone of her voice, but my throat dries up at the mention of my girlfriend. What does she want from Maddy now?

"I didn't know that who I am friends with is

any of your business, Gia," Gianna responds with the same amount of sass and snark as Gia. The guys hoot, and Jared chuckles, draping an arm over Gianna's shoulder and pulling her closer to him.

I feel a pang of jealousy at such a blatant public display of affection. I wish I could have that with Madeline. I wish I could bring her out with my friends and show her off. I wish I could be cozy with her in front of them and not be worried about someone coming for her in the next moment. I push the feelings away just as Gia responds, "She is a wannabe whore. I don't know what you are doing keeping company with such lowlifes."

I clench my hands into fists at her words. I knew I should not have come to lunch with these people when Gia was going to accompany us.

"At least she respects the people around her, especially her friends," Gianna snaps, and I am grateful for her standing up for my girlfriend. I feel ashamed of myself for not saying anything, but I am scared that one word from me will have my secret spilling out into public.

"First of all, you are not my friend. The guys and I only tolerate you because you are Jared's little plaything. Second of all, I know why you are friends with a lowlife like Madeline. You know, being promiscuous and all..." Gia waves around, glancing around the table as if she expects anyone to laugh.

None of the guys even smile at her comment because they know how much Gianna means to Jared. The man is in love with her, and calling his girlfriend promiscuous in front of the whole group...Gia messed up.

Gianna grits her teeth and gets up from her seat, slamming her hands on the table. "Maddy is my friend, and I won't hear you saying anything about her. And we all know why you are friends with the guys. You want to get into Steven's pants, but guess what? He actually has taste and ignores you, just as he should." She seethes before storming out of the diner.

Jared turns to Gia, whose face has gone ashen. I feel the others' eyes on me but don't look up to meet their gazes. Dammit. "If you call my girlfriend promiscuous one more time, Gia, it won't end well for you. And I mean every word." Jared snaps at her, his voice low and menacing.

He follows his girlfriend out of the diner, and everyone grows silent. Gia glances at the couple who have just left over her shoulder before rolling her eyes and turning to look at us, a smile on her lips.

"Some people are so sensitive; it's

embarrassing," she lets out a laugh, and her minions join her this time. I glance at Logan, who rolls his eyes, done with this bullshit.

"You are a fucking bitch for what you said to Gianna," he says, turning to Gia, his voice a lazy drawl. "And also what you did to Maddy. That was a shit move," he adds.

I feel relief flood through my chest at someone finally calling out Gia. I would have preferred it to be me, but my hands are tied. Gia's face turns red as she leaves her seat too, telling her friends to follow her. She walks out and we let out a sigh of relief.

"The woman's a menace, but she knows her stuff in bed," Nick comments, and I roll my eyes. The others chuckle, and we all turn to our food. The atmosphere lightens as the moments pass by. I knew something like this would go down when I spotted Maddy in the bleachers with Gianna.

I am glad she has at least one friend in my group. I am glad that not all my friends are asses. As we finish our lunch and walk out of the diner, Logan claps me on the shoulder and catches up to me. Leaning forward, he says in a low tone, "When are you planning to tell the group that the woman they are talking about on the daily is actually your girlfriend?"

I freeze, feeling the color drain from my face. I turn to glance at him to find him grinning at me like a fool. I don't know what to be more surprised at, the grin on Logan's face or the fact that he knows about Madeline and me.

"I don't know what you mean," I shake my head as I resume walking again, trying to shake off the initial shock that I felt.

"Come on, man. You don't need to hide it from me. I know what is going on with Maddy and you. Jared and Gianna do, too," Logan says, and I jerk my head to the side to look at him.

"Who else knows about this rumor?" I ask, not confirming anything until I know where they stand in this situation.

"No one. Especially not Gia," his expression softens slightly, and I swallow, looking away. I want to tell him then that I am in a relationship with Maddy, probably falling in love with her utterly and completely. But I don't dare to speak.

"I don't know what you guys are on, but you are crazy," I answer instead as I walk away from him and get into my car. I turn on the engine and pull out of the parking lot, my head reeling from the possibility of the others knowing about Maddy and me.

***

A few hours later, when I walk into the living room, Maddy is curled up on the couch, watching a movie. I plop down next to her and wrap an arm around her. She turns and smiles at me, kissing me before turning her attention back to the television.

"There is a party this weekend," she says as she watches the movie. "I am going with Emma and Lenny." She gives me a sideways glance, and I let out a sigh.

"What do you want me to say, Mads? You know I can't take you," I tell her. She grimaces as she turns to look at me.

"You don't want to take me," she says, pulling away from me and putting several inches of distance between us.

"Whatever is that supposed to mean?" I ask her. We have fought in the past, Maddy and I. In the two months, now turning three, that we have been together, we have fought several times. Even before that, we used to get into arguments, but she has never looked so angry.

"Are you embarrassed of being seen with me, Steve?" She frowns, and her gaze turns sad.

"No, of course not. You know very well why I can't take you with me, why we can't be seen together," I reason with her. We had come to a mutual agreement. I hadn't forced her to be in a secret relationship with me. It had been both of our decisions.

"Yes, I do get that. But I have been thinking about it... and why do we care about Gia? Why does she hold so much power over us? We can very well be in a relationship, announce it to the public and ignore her like we do now." She raises her eyebrows at me, her expression turning hopeful.

My stomach twists with discomfort. "Mads, you know that we can't do that. We decided to keep our relationship a secret until we got out of university. What has changed now?" I ask, not understanding why for the life of me she would want to suddenly turn our relationship public.

"I was scared of Gia back then. I talked to Gianna the other day. She told me that Logan, Jared, and she have been speculating that we are in a relationship. Your friends already know. Why not confirm it?" She questions.

"I just can't," I snap, getting up from the couch and facing her. Maddy seems startled, her eyes wide and her mouth open. I realize that I raised my voice at her, but the anger spreading through my chest makes me go on, even though I know that I should stop. "I can't. I don't know why you don't understand that. I thought you got into this relationship knowing what I can and cannot offer you. I can't afford to show you around the university because everyone will come for me, Maddy! Don't you understand that?!"

I realize a beat too laten what I actually said. I realize that I did admit to my real reason for wanting to keep the relationship a secret. I am concerned about Maddy's safety and her reputation, but more than that, I am concerned for mine.

"So, you are ashamed to be seen with me," Maddy mutters under her breath, low enough that if the living room were not so silent, I wouldn't have heard her. "You were not concerned about me, Steven. You were only worried about yourself because I am an embarrassment to be seen with, because you are so high on the social ladder that having a girlfriend who isn't on the same level, is humiliating to you."

Maddy gets up from the couch, and I rub my face, exhaustion starting to weigh on my shoulders. I know I have hurt her, but I don't know what to do now. I have spilled the truth. But I do like her. I like her a lot.

"Mads, listen to me—" I step closer to her, putting my hands on her arms, but she shakes them off, her expression turning thunderous.

"Do not call me Mads. You have lost all your rights," she snaps, but then when she speaks next, her voice cracks. "You said that Gia was wrong that night, that she has been wrong every time she insulted me, but guess what, Steven? Her words never hurt as much as yours does right now because it proves that you agree with her. You agree with everything she said about me." Tears fall from her eyes, and I feel my heart clench painfully in my chest. No, no, no, no. I didn't wanted to hurt her.

"Maddy, no. I don't agree with her," I respond, my voice turning pleading.

"You don't? Put it in your story right now that we are in a relationship. Post our picture on your Instagram, take me out to meet your friends, and be my date to the party this weekend. Can you do that?" She asks, baring her teeth at me.

I turn her words over in my head. I want to say yes. I want to tell her that I don't care about my reputation as much as I care about her, but the words clog my throat. I open my mouth to speak, but they don't come out. My silence kills me, and from the looks of it, it is killing her too. But should I lie to her? She deserves someone who is not a coward, and that person isn't me. So, I stay quiet. Maybe we were not meant to be after all.

"Very well then," Maddy's voice is a whimper, the tears pouring over her face. I want to wipe them away, but I stay put, my resolve strengthening. She deserves better. So much better.

"This secret relationship is done for, Steven. We," she waves a hand between the two of us, and I hear my heart cracking in my chest. "...are done." She finishes, and my heart shatters.

***

CHAPTER TWENTY-FIVE

Madeline Scott

I walk into the cafe the next morning, my head and eyes hurting from crying all night. I don't know how the tears stopped, but they did at some point. I have never cried so much in my entire life. It feels as if every bad thing that I had thought about myself and forced myself to be, just because I believe in being your most authentic self, has backfired.

Riya glances at me when I walk up to the front counter, her eyebrows climbing higher on her forehead. "Maddy, are you okay?" she asks, but I just nod at her, unable to muster the smile that I would usually give her.

I didn't run into Steven when I woke up this morning, and I am grateful. My heart was beating the whole time I ate my breakfast and got ready for work, but thankfully, he didn't come out of his room, or maybe he had already left. I don't know.

"Maddy?" Riya calls my name again, and I turn to look at her, my expression turning sour.

"What do you want?" I snap, unable to keep the edge from my voice. Her eyes widen at my sudden outburst, but I can't bring myself to care.

I look away and turn back to arranging the pastries on the display.

I am yet to tell Emma that my relationship has come to an end, that it had been a scam of sorts, that I got played. Steven's words keep ringing in my ears. He was worried about his reputation, what people would think when they saw him with me. I get that I am not the ideal girlfriend, that I am not the woman guys usually go for.

I am not quirky or weird or confident or sexy. I am just… me. I don't know how to describe it, but guys run away from me. I think that was the reason my ex cheated on me.

I don't know how I manage to go about my routine, but I find myself working all through the morning as if I have been put on auto-pilot. I don't smile at the regular customers, and I can see the disappointment reflected in their eyes, but I don't care.

I thought a lot last night. When I couldn't cry

anymore, I let myself think. I thought about myself and all my values and what I believed to be true. And I have come to the conclusion that the world is not a nice place for those who dare to be themselves. People will have no problem being with a person who is rotten to the core, but they will be scared, to be seen with someone who is authentic and kind.

The world is not kind to kind people, to people who have a good heart. I thought someday, I could change the way people look at me. I thought that maybe one day, they will look at me and not settle their judgements on me. But what does it say about the world when my boyfriend, who claimed to have been pining over me for years, thinks that I am an embarrassment to be seen with because others don't appreciate me for who I am. But he has no problem being seen in public with Gia, who is known to be a monster through and through.

"Hey, that's not my order," a lady cries out as she stares at the bag I put on the counter.

"I'm sorry?" I ask as I take a look inside the bag she hands back to me with a glare settled on me. A blueberry muffin is inside, and I turn to the computer to see what her order was. I sigh as I realize I put a blueberry muffin in her order instead of a chocolate chip muffin.

"I am sorry; I will get your order right," I apologize and turn to the display to retrieve her chocolate chip muffin when she says, "You have one job. How hard can it be?"

The leash on my anger that I have been barely controlling since last night snaps, and I whirl to look at the woman. "Excuse me, ma'am. I apologized for getting your order wrong. I would appreciate it if you just shut your mouth and let me do my job. I am very sorry, but my job is not to put up with a nasty personality," I answer, my voice turning vicious.

The woman looks around, offended, before she begins to call me names. I feel my anger growing and am ready to give her a piece of my mind when Riya steps up, intervening.

"I am so sorry, ma'am. We will get you your order," she turns to the new girl and gestures for her to take over the front counter.

"Come with me," she says to me, tugging on my arm and dragging me to the back room.

Once inside, she closes the door behind herself and turns to me, disappointment etched on her face. "I don't know what is going on with you today, Maddy, but you need to calm down. I suggest that you take the rest of the day off. I will let Lisa know that you are sick."

"But I am not sick," I protest, but she puts up a hand, stopping me.

"You are not sick, but it is clear that you are not in the right state of mind to be dealing with customers today. It will be better if you take the rest of the morning off," she says sternly, and I feel exhaustion weighing down on my shoulders. I want to sleep again. I nod my head and pull the apron over my head, walking out of the cafe without putting it on the hook. I let the tears fall once I am walking down the street and feel as if I will burst if I don't cry now.

***

Emma was furious when she found out about my breakup. I went over to her dorm room after classes were over and curled up on her bed, sleeping off my sadness. My best friend let me, not pushing me to talk about how I felt. I didn't feel like anything.

Every ounce of happiness that I had found over the last few months seemed to have been snatched away from me, leaving me empty-handed. I didn't like this void in my chest, but it was there. I didn't like the fact that Steven looked as good as ever either. I saw him with his friends this morning, and he was laughing with them. It felt like a gut punch to the heart.

I thought that maybe he would fight for us, that maybe he would change and tell me that he would make our relationship public and that I didn't need to worry. But he looked as happy as ever, as unbothered as ever. When our eyes met earlier today, he was the first one to look away, glancing and smiling at Gia, who gladly walked to his side and cozied up to him.

I clenched my teeth as the scene replayed itself in my head. I should have known how badly our relationship would end. I blamed myself for thinking that maybe I could have my happily ever after. I should have known that I couldn't have it.

"Maddy, stop crying," Emma consoled me, stroking my hair, which was sticking to my forehead and my tear-stained cheeks.

"I am not crying," I said, damn well knowing that I hadn't been able to stop since I started half an hour ago.

"He doesn't deserve you. He is an ass for making you feel this way." She kissed the top of my head, and I shook my head, whimpering.

"He thinks I am everything that Gia said I was. He can bear being seen with her in public but not me. What does it say about me, Em? Am I worse than Gia?" I asked the questions that I desperately needed an answer to. I wanted to know what was so wrong with me, that a guy couldn't fathom being seen with me.

"Nothing is wrong with you, Maddy," someone said, and it was not Emma. I raised my head to find Gianna standing at the foot of Emma's bed, with a sad expression. She walked over to me and perched on the bed.

I managed to get up and sit, wiping at my tears because it looked unflattering. "Oh, come on, I know what everyone thinks, Gianna. You don't need to sugarcoat the truth." I rolled my eyes as I felt another cry bubble up in my chest.

"The people who think that there is something wrong with you are cowards, Maddy," Gianna says, and Emma nods in agreement, taking a seat beside her.

"You are the realest person I know. You encourage and inspire so many of us on the daily.

Why do you think you have so many followers on Instagram, love?" Gianna asks.

"Because I am pretty?" I ask, letting out a chuckle. My friends crack a smile, but Gianna shakes her head, taking my hand in hers.

"No, because you are real. You are exactly like you are in real life and online. You are loving and beautiful and love everything and everyone. It is your strength. Don't let others convince you that it is a weakness." She squeezes my hand, and I let out a small smile.

My lips wobble, though, and I am reminded of Steven's words once again. How can I not think of my strength as my weakness when I lost someone so special to me, because of it?

"The person who has lost you is one hell of a jerk, because he let you go," Gianna goes on.

"And you don't have to beat yourself up for him, Maddy. We all love you, okay? And I am sure the one who is truly meant for you, will love you the way we do," Emma adds, scooting closer to me and embracing me. Gianna follows suit, and I wonder if she knows that Steven and I have broken up. It did seem so from the way she was speaking, but I don't want to assume it.

I let my friends hug me and give me some much-needed comfort. I know I will not be able to look at myself the same for a while, but I do appreciate them trying to make me feel better. I close my eyes and breathe deeply, adamant about not wanting to cry again.

I will not cry over Steven anymore; I promise myself. I pull away from my friends, smiling at them. "I appreciate you guys wanting to make me feel better, but I would feel much, much better if we can go out for some ice cream and coffee," I say.

Gianna and Emma grin at each other before getting off of the bed, pulling me up. "What are we waiting for then?" Emma asks.

"Maybe wash your face before we go?" Gianna suggests, and I roll my eyes, but I walk out of the room anyway because I know she is right. I look like a bruised peach, and I am self-aware enough to admit it. I need to get over Steven, and I know it is going to be hard because, believe it or not, I was falling in love with him. But I will get over him, one way or another.

I have never let people who don't like me, get to me before. I am not going to let one man get to me now. I am not someone who lets others disrespect her, and even if I don't love myself at the moment, I will not insult myself by abandoning myself. So, I walk into the common bathroom and freshen up. When I walk out, Emma and Gianna are waiting for me, smiles on their faces, and the latter's car keys dangling from her fingers.

***

CHAPTER TWENTY-SIX

STEVEN JONES

I pull a fresh shirt over my head, picking up the towel and drying my hair. The guys chat amongst themselves, but I am not paying any attention to them, or rather, was not paying attention to them until Jared mentions Maddy.

"Gianna is out with Maddy and Emma. She won't join us today," my friend says as he gets into his clothes and begins packing up. "Apparently,

Maddy is going through a breakup." He glances at me briefly, but I look away, pretending to appear busy.

"Really? Who has she been dating?" Logan asks, his voice unnaturally high. I know what the fucker is trying to do, and I am not going to fall for it.

"The guy has to be one real jerk to let her go, though," Jared shrugs, and I grit my teeth. Are they my friends or Maddy's?

"Maddy was dating someone? Damn. After what Gia did, I doubt any man would want to get with her," Nick comments, shaking his head. He looks immensely amused with his shitty joke, and I want to punch him.

"Maybe she was dating him before Gia's little prank. And maybe he finally came to his senses and left her," another guy says, chuckling a little. Nick joins him, and I feel myself getting angry all over again for an entirely different reason.

"Hey guys, I am heading home," I tell the guys and walk out of the room before anyone can stop me. I don't want to talk about Maddy or hear others talk about her.

The guys are suspicious of me being the one Maddy was dating. And Jared is right; I am a jerk for letting her go, but I am too much of a coward for her. I can't accept her completely, can't tell the world that she is the woman I love, that I chose for me. Hell, I can't even tell my own parents that Madeline is my girlfriend, that she is the girl I want to be with. Or rather was my girlfriend.

I drive all the way back to the house in a daze. I don't know what I will do if I run into Maddy. I left today before she was up. I didn't want to run into her, and I was lucky enough to have escaped her in the morning. Now that I walk into the house, I hold my breath, listening for any sounds.

It seems though, Jared was right, and she must be still out with Gianna and Emma. I wish I was like Gianna, who could stand up to Gia and the others who I know will have a problem with my relationship. I wish I could be the man I wished I could be, for Maddy's sake, but I am not Gianna, and instead I hurt Maddy and made her break up with me.

I go to my room and close the door, locking the whole world out. I don't want to deal with anyone right now. I want to wallow in self-pity for a while. I want to hate myself a little.

***

The days blur together after my break up with Maddy. She continues to live in the house, minding her own business and keeping her distance. She doesn't pay me any attention, even if I happen to be in the kitchen or the dining room at the same time as her. She pointedly ignores me all the time, and I think it is the best for both of us. I don't think I will be able to meet her eyes, even if she decides to talk to me.

We keep to our own rooms, and the time we used to spend together fades into a memory. I feel my misery grow once more and more, with each day that passes, and we are not together. I become the shell of a man that I once used to be, before she came to live with me.

I sit down at the dinner table today and wait for Maddy to come in, but she doesn't. I keep waiting for her, but she doesn't show up. When I am almost done with dinner, the door to the dining room opens, and Maddy walks in. She pushes an envelope toward me and says, "I am moving out.

This is your rent for this month. Thank you for letting me stay here for as long as I did."

I turn to face her, but it is not her words that surprise me more. It is the fact that she has her hair down, thin braids pulling her hair away from her scalp. I stare at her for a moment, not knowing how to react. I have always wanted to see her with her hair down, but I never thought that it would be under these circumstances when I can't even tell her what a goddess she is.

"Where are you going?" I ask, finding my voice finally. My gaze flickers to the envelope, and I feel something tighten in my chest.

"I think that isn't something that concerns you. In fact, I am leaving right now. The movers are here," she informs me, turning around and walking out of the door. I put my spoon down on my plate and get up, following her. Movers walk up and down the stairs as they carry her things out of her room. I don't want her to go, but I don't think it would be fair to ask her to stay when I couldn't give her what she asked of me.

I shake my head as I walk back into the dining room, unable to watch her leave me behind for good. The year is coming to an end already, and it seems like my heart is ripping apart at the thought of never seeing Maddy again.

I force myself to sit down in my chair and shove spoonful of rice into my mouth, ignoring the way it seemed that Maddy was taking away my peace and sanity along with her.

I only come out of the dining room when I am sure that the movers have left, and Maddy has gone with them. I don't dare to come out before the house is empty and silent. A heaviness starts to weigh down on my shoulders as I realize that perhaps, this was the last time that I will have ever talked to Maddy.

I walk to my room and get into bed, not wanting to face the world for some time. I want to disappear, but that is not possible, so I just get under my covers and decide to go to sleep. I close my eyes, but sleep wouldn't come to me. It is within my reach, weighing down my eyelids and making me feel tired, but I can't get any closer to it than that.

I toss and turn for some time, but nothing happens. My life seems to have changed for the worst, ever since I made the decision to let Maddy break up with me and move on for the better. I am sure that she will find someone better, but I am not sure that I will find mine.

There is no way that I can. Maddy was the best I could have ever wished for, and I messed up my chances with her.

My phone rings, and I groan, raising my head and reaching for it from the nightstand. I glance at the screen to find my father calling. I answer the call and bring the device to my ear, wanting to be done with this conversation already, when it hasn't even started yet.

"Hello, Steven," my father says, and I feel my breathing turning shallow. His voice is a reminder of what I have lost, what I will never have again. It is a reminder of the coward I am and how I don't deserve to be with anyone. When I couldn't do justice to the woman I love. The woman who loved me.

"Dad, I will talk to you later," I choke the words out before hanging up. Placing the phone back on the nightstand, I get up because my chest is getting more choked by the moment. I swallow, but it doesn't seem better.

My heart starts to beat faster with every moment that goes by. My hands shake as I bring them up to rub my face. The silence of the house presses in on me, making me want to scream and disappear. I feel the heaviness in my chest grow heavier and heavier until I can't breathe anymore.

I stumble out of my bed and walk over to the window, throwing it open, but I still can't breathe. I feel my vision turning hazy, and my heart kicks into panic. I reach for my phone and open my contacts, dialing Logan's number. I don't think I can talk to anyone else at the moment. The only other person has left my life for good, just minutes ago.

"Steve?" Logan's voice came in through the speaker, and I felt a wave of relief. But the dwindling supply of air quickly replaced it with panic once more.

"Can you come over?" I managed to push the words out of my throat. I had never asked my friends to come over, but I didn't think I could handle myself on my own.

"Are you alright, Steve? You don't sound too good." I could almost see my friend frowning on the other end of the line.

"No, no. I am not alright. Just…come." I let the phone slip from my hand as I sank down to the floor. Clutching my knees to my chest, I tried to calm myself down. I had never felt like this before. I had never felt a fear so profound, never wanted to escape my own skin like I did now.

I waited for Logan to arrive. I didn't know how much time passed before I heard the door to my room open. I heard footsteps, and then Logan was kneeling in front of me. I was glad to see him. I wanted to tell him that I was happy to see him, but the words wouldn't come out.

"She left," I said instead when I opened my mouth, "She left me."

"Come on, Steve. Let's get you on the bed." My friend put a hand on my shoulder, trying to get me to stand up, but I didn't budge. I stopped him with a hand on his and turned pleading eyes on him.

"She left, Lo. She will never come back again." I was shaking. I was aware of the way my body was shaking, and I felt like I was spiraling, but I didn't know how to make it stop. I just knew that Maddy was no longer a part of my life, and the thought gutted me.

"Steve, you are having a panic attack. I need

you to try to breathe, okay? Focus," Logan replied, trying to get me to breathe as he gestured for me to inhale and exhale.

I shook my head, finding the exercise irrelevant. "Maddy left, Lo. She left because I couldn't give her what she wanted." I shook my head.

"We will talk about it, Steve. I promise. But I want you to breathe first," he pleaded, and this time, I allowed myself to obey him.

I followed his lead as he instructed me to inhale, hold, and exhale. My chest started to loosen as I continued breathing, and I felt my head starting to clear too. My breathing returned to normal, albeit slowly, and I stopped shaking.

When I was no longer in a fit of panic, I spoke again. "I lost her, Lo. What do I do now?" I asked him.

My friend blinked at me for a moment before reaching forward and wrapping his arms around my neck.

"You gotta apologize, man. You gotta tell her that she was enough," he answered, and when he pulled away, I wondered if he had lost a woman he loved, too. I wondered if Logan was so cold-hearted not because he was not capable of emotions but because he had had a woman walk out on him, too.

***

CHAPTER TWENTY-SEVEN

Madeline Scott

My new apartment is nowhere near as fancy as Steven's house. In fact, it isn't fancy at all, and I find myself missing Steven and his house at times, not because of the facilities that his house provided, but because of the company Steven provided. It has been a struggle trying to get into a routine that doesn't include him.

We were together for three months, but I had

been living with him for six. I had become used to the house, had become used to the feeling of living in it. And now that it's all gone, I find myself wanting it, reaching for it every chance I get.

I chew on the end of my pencil, staring at the assignment laid out in front of me. I am stressed, to say the least, because the assignment is due in two days, and I'm afraid that I won't be able to get it done. I close my eyes as I inhale, telling myself that I will be able to get it done if I just concentrate for a few moments.

I open my eyes and focus on my assignment, pushing all the thoughts out of my head for the moment. I begin to write once more before turning to my laptop and typing down the assignment, taking help from the notes I have jotted down.

I find a flow soon enough, and then I don't

feel pressured anymore, typing and retyping the assignment until I have completed it. I sigh in relief, leaning back in my seat once I am done, and stare at the screen in front of me. I plan on getting it edited tomorrow and submitting it. I will need at least a day to go through it again.

I decide to take a break as I get out of my chair and walk into my kitchen to make myself a cup of coffee. My love for coffee is the only thing that hasn't changed, even after I broke up with Steven and moved out of his house.

Coffee is an antidote to my sorrows and my guilt. It is a way to forget about my worries and focus on my future. And right now, I am focused on getting good grades in my finals. I have started studying more vigorously than before, and since I don't have anyone to distract me with kisses along the column of my neck, I get a lot more done than I could before.

I don't allow myself to think too much about Steven. I don't allow myself to dwell on the way we ended things and how easily he moved on from me when I was struggling to wake up every day and go about my routine. My friends have stopped mentioning him, and it feels as if my crush on him, was a lifetime ago.

I hate this part of relationships when you have to forget about all the good and bad times and move on in hopes that you find something better. What if I want what I had? What if happiness is in staying in the past and reliving the good memories?

I wonder if Steven thinks about me. I do know that I am the one who broke things off and moved out, but he didn't stop me either. I wonder if he thinks he made a mistake and if he regrets not fighting for me, for us.

I shake my head as I prepare my coffee,

reminding myself of the promise I have made to myself. I will focus on myself and leave the past behind me where it belongs. I want to become an actor, and that is what I am going to focus on. I have no place in my life for unnecessary stress like that of having a man in my life and stressing over the well-being of our relationship.

I am not anti-relationships all of a sudden. I just don't feel like I need it right now. I want to live life and not think about the heartbreak I went through. I want to enjoy myself and find myself once more. I seem to have lost the girl I used to be, the one others looked at and smiled, felt inspired by, like Gianna said.

I need to get that girl back, no matter how out of my reach she might feel. I am never giving up on her, ever.

***

Emma and I sit in the cafeteria across from each other, eating our food in silence. Ever since my breakup, our lunches have been pretty dry because I have not been in the mood to talk, and my best friend is too scared to say the wrong thing in my presence. I don't know when I became the person people had to think twice before speaking to, but I am not loving it at all.

"I was thinking about going to the party this weekend. It is the last one before finals start, and we are going to have a blast!" I say as I look up at Emma.

She glances at me, a smile making its way onto her face like it does every time now that I look in a good mood. I feel a pang of sympathy for her to have to be so cautious around me, but I am working on it.

"That is a great idea! I think you should go out

and enjoy yourself," she responds, and I nod my head, taking another bite of my salad.

"I want to live the full college experience. I am not going to back down now just because a guy broke my heart." I roll my eyes with a sass that I don't feel. I am aware that Steven is sitting a few tables away from me with his friends.

Gia is sitting right beside him, seeming to have cozied up to him since our breakup. I don't know how I feel about him moving onto her, from me. I mean, it definitely sucks, but am I really surprised?

No, I am just a little hurt. But I can have fun, too, can't I? I can bag a guy, too.

My gaze flickers over to Logan, who is sitting on Steven's other side. I know I am being an ass, going for my ex's best friend, but can you blame me? Steven hurt me. I want someone to make me forget about the hurt.

"Oh, hell no." Emma's voice makes me turn to face her. She is shaking her head, her lips pressing into a hard line. "Don't even think about Logan," she adds.

"Why not?" I frown.

"You don't go for your ex's best friend. That's not nice!" Emma says.

I roll my eyes, leaning back in my seat. "I doubt that it is a rule, Emma. I am going to be at a party, and I am going to enjoy myself with any guy who catches my interest." I smirk, flicking my gaze over to the group once more. None of them look at me, and I am glad. I am done being scared of them. I will be like them now. Life of the party.

***

The party is full of activity. I don't know who threw it, but it is lit. I walk through the crowd, Emma in tow as I look for my target for the night. My best friend's hand tightens around my arm as I spot the group of friends standing far off in the corner.

I am eager to get to them, or rather get to Logan, who is standing in a corner with a drink in hand. He is scanning the place with disinterest, and I know I have chosen the right guy. Steven, on the other hand, is standing with the rest of the group, Gia leaning into him. I wonder if they are dating. I don't care, I remind myself.

"I still don't think you should do this," Emma says into my ear, her voice loud over the music. "It is such a dick move, Maddy," she adds.

I roll my eyes at her, still convinced that I need to get myself a rebound to make myself feel better.

Maybe I am being stupid, but I don't care as long as I get what I want, that is, getting over Steven. I want to know that other men out there can take care of my needs, in whom I can lose myself.

"It's going to be okay," I tell Emma, pulling her hand away from my arm as I walk over to Logan. His eyes find mine as I approach him, and he pauses, his glass paused halfway to his mouth.

I know I look good tonight with my shorts and a see-through top with a bralette underneath. My hair is down, a crown of braids on the top of my head, and a little glitter makeup to complete the look. "Care to dance with me?" I ask Logan, gesturing over my shoulder at the dance floor, pumping with music and sweaty bodies grinding against each other.

Logan's eyes raise over my shoulder, and I turn around to find Steven and Gia staring at us, or rather, Steven is staring and Gia is trying to get him to listen to her. I peel my gaze away from my ex, feeling a pang in my heart that seems to consume me.

"Logan?" I wave a hand in front of Logan's face, and he looks at me finally. "Dance with me?" I ask again, offering him my hand.

He stares at it for a moment, looking at Steven once more before nodding and taking it. Placing the cup on the table beside him, he leads me onto the dance floor. I feel the music pumping through me as his hands find my waist, pulling me closer to him.

I put my hand on his shoulders, letting myself feel the muscles underneath as I let him guide me through the steps. I would have loved to dance with Steven, but too bad he is embarrassed to be seen with me. I ignore the anger bubbling in my chest as I focus on Logan's arms on my waist, pulling me closer to him. I let him, tilting my head to the side as he nuzzles the column of my neck, making heat spread through my body.

He pushes me away from him before pulling back, and I press my body against his. I am supposed to enjoy this, I remind myself as I let Logan guide me through the steps of the dance. Our steps get continuously lewd, and I feel the crowd around us pausing to look at us.

Logan flicks out his tongue, tracing the length of my jaw and collarbone, making me melt into his arms. My eyes flutter shut, and I feel myself needing to get closer to him, wanting to feel him all over me. I know the others are watching us intently now, but I can't bring myself to care. I want to forget the world. I want to forget Steven. And I want to forget the way my heart aches in my chest.

I am still lost in Logan's arms, the way he makes good use of his mouth and his tongue, that I don't notice that someone is watching us. Or rather approaching us. Logan's mouth flutters over my lips, and I arch my neck, trying to capture his, but before I can kiss him fully on the lips, he is being wrenched away from me.

"You fucking asshole!" I open my eyes to see Steven seething as he punches Logan in the jaw. Horror unfurls in my chest, and I bring a hand to my mouth, the temperature in my body dropping a few degrees.

***

CHAPTER TWENTY-EIGHT

Steven Jones

I can't see straight as I punch Logan in the jaw once more. The bastard dares to grin at me as I swing another blow at him. My anger clouds my vision, and I can't bring myself to stop. He touched her. He almost kissed her. He knows that I love her. He knows that she is mine.

"How could you do this to me, Logan?" I demand, taking a step toward him. I raise my fist once more, but someone grabs it, the touch making me pause. I've been needing to feel it ever since she broke up with me a few weeks ago.

"What the hell do you think you're doing?" Maddy asks, her voice ringing with anger. She doesn't get to be angry at this. I should be the angry one.

"How dare he touch you?" I ask, whirling to face her. I am aware that everyone is watching me. I am aware that everyone is witnessing this madness, but I can't bring myself to care. I don't want another guy touching Maddy. I know I said she deserves someone better than me, but I can't let her be anybody else's. I can't.

"What do you mean, huh?" She asks, her nostrils flaring. "You were the one who was ashamed of being with me in public. Not every guy is a fucking coward like you, Steven. If you won't give me what I want, someone else will. Your friend is willing to give it to me." She snaps.

"I think you have a thing for making scenes at parties," Gia steps up, her voice sharp as she glances between Maddy and me. "I suggest you leave with your boy toy and let us all enjoy our night." She adds, and Maddy smiles, for once not annoyed by her suggestion.

"Good idea." She sidesteps me and walks to Logan's side. A bruise is forming on his jaw, and I have to refrain from doing more damage than I have already done.

"I am down," he grins at her, taking her hand in his, and I swallow. I will fucking kill the bastard.

"What the fuck do you think you are doing, huh?" I demand, getting away from Gia, whom I want to punch too.

"Getting out of here with my boy toy," Maddy raises herself on her tiptoes and kisses Logan on the cheek. She is pissing me off, and I hate being messed with.

"I have been waiting for this night for some time now," Logan chuckles, wrapping an arm around her bare waist and pulling her into his side. She smiles at him and watches from the corner of her eye as I walk up to them.

I grab her arm and pull her away from Logan, making her scowl at me. "Steven, you are putting up a shitshow for no reason at all. We are over. You can't be with me all the time, and I am tired of being your little secret. I need a guy who is not fucking ashamed of me," she says, hissing out each word as she tries to get her hand out of my grip.

"We are not over," I respond. I am not done with her. I have never been done with her, and I doubt I will ever be fine letting her go. "You decided to walk away. But I am not done with you," I add.

"You don't get to do this to me. It is either accepting me in front of the world or just forgetting about me," she all but screams.

"This is a very public fight for no reason at all. Let's get out of here," I tell her, tugging on her arm and making her walk away from the group.

"Steven, what are you doing?" Gia calls my name, and I wonder if she doesn't understand even now that she is not the one I am interested in. I love Maddy, and she is the one I am going to be with. End of the story.

"I don't want to talk to you," Maddy protests, trying to get her hand out of my grip, but I refuse to let go. She is going to listen to me out, and we are going to sort this shit out between ourselves. I need her to be with me. I can't live without her, for fuck's sake.

"But I need to talk to you," I respond as I pull her into an empty room and lock the door behind us.

I turn to face her, only to find her standing with her hands crossed over her chest and a venomous expression on her face.

"I don't want to listen to what you have to say," she spits out. I have never seen her so annoyed at me, but she has to know that I made a mistake and that I can't live without her. Fuck, I almost died when she left me.

"Please, Mads. Let me explain myself to you," I plead. She searches my face, her eyes narrowing slightly. I don't know what she is thinking, but I hope she lets me redeem myself, that she gives me another chance. "I need to tell you something. Please," I beg.

Maddy swallows then and nods her head as if her resolve is weakening. Stepping away from me, she leans against a wall, unfolding her arms from her chest.

"Go ahead. But this better be worth my time, Jones, or I will kick your ass for cock-blocking me," she snaps, and I try not to think about Logan and her together.

I don't know what Logan was trying to achieve tonight, but the bastard did manage to make me grow some balls. I will be questioning him later, though. But first, I need to win my girl back.

"I know I was an ass to you during our relationship, Maddy. I know I probably shouldn't even be given this chance to explain myself, but I need you to know that the problem was not with you but me," I begin, lowering my head as I feel the shame weighing down on my shoulders. I got to know from Gianna that Maddy was blaming herself for the breakup and that she thought that her being who she was the reason I felt ashamed for being in a relationship with her.

"All my life, I have been living by others' rules. I do what others expect me to do, and I am who others want me to be. I am just a puppet. Or rather, I used to be. I used to go along with the expectations other people had of me. I always acted the way they wanted me to act. The only reason I was an ass to most people was because I felt like that as a jock, I had to be one," I inhale, pausing.

"I thought that if I didn't act the way others expected me to, I would never fit in. I did what I thought was acceptable, and I didn't do what I thought people wouldn't like. But along the way, I forgot who I was. I forgot who Steven Jones was. Other than being a soccer player and a womanizer, I was nothing. I couldn't describe myself for the life of me. I fell into a deep depression that, it was hard for me to even get out of bed in the morning. My parents didn't care because as long as they got what they wanted from me, a soccer champion and a good student, I was doing good." I pause once more, trying to find the courage to continue.

I dare to look at Maddy to find her listening to me attentively. Her expression doesn't give away what she is thinking or what she feels about the whole situation. I want her to speak, but I know I should finish my part before letting her say hers.

"I set out to look for a roommate because I couldn't bear to be alone anymore. I wanted someone with whom I could be the real me, because I desperately needed someone who understood me and who wouldn't shy away from me and cut me off if I tried to express myself. I found that person in you, Maddy."

"When I asked you to move in with me, I didn't want you just because you were my crush for the last three years, but because I knew you to be the only one with a heart that didn't judge and love endlessly. I knew that you would never look at me and cringe away from the darkness because you never shied away from people when they were sad, angry, or in despair."

"When I said that you taught me how to smile, Mads, I meant it. You brought me back a happiness that I didn't know I could experience. You brought with you a life that I would enjoy living. And I was so grateful for it. But then I messed up. I know I should have put our relationship out into the world right from the start or even from when you asked me to. I know I should have granted you your wish because you deserve to be shown off. But I got scared, Mads. I was scared that the others would rip me apart if I put our relationship out in public."

"But when I lost you...it was worse than the insults that I would have experienced otherwise. After you were gone, I realized just how pathetic I have become, how stupid I was to let go of something real, for something that has been fake right from the very start. When I lost you, Mads, my life stopped being something to enjoy, to dance through once again."

"I know I have hurt you deeply, that I have brought your worst fears to life and even made you hate yourself, but I want you to give me a second chance. I am so sorry, Maddy. I am so sorry to have hurt you, to have treated you less than how you deserve to be treated. But I can't live without you.

I can't breathe when you're not around. I love you. I love you so much that it is the only thing that is keeping me alive. So I beg for this second chance and hope you grant me it." And with that, I lower myself onto my knees, joining my hands in front of her.

I don't care that I am sacrificing my pride and ego. I don't care that I probably look pathetic at the moment. But I need to let her know that I love her. That I am willing to beg for her forgiveness, for another chance with her. Seeing her with Logan today made me realize how she must have felt, watching me with Gia. It made me realize that no matter how much I console myself or convince myself, I will always love Maddy. I will always want her. And I can't bear to see her with another man.

I keep my gaze lowered, unable to look her in the eye. I have never felt so ashamed of myself. I have never wanted to hate myself but I do now.

Logan was willing to be the man Maddy deserves, and he doesn't even love her. Can't I do the same? Why do I care so much about the world? I shouldn't. Maddy is my love and she is the only one I care for.

"You made me hate myself, Steve," Maddy speaks up after a long time. Her words hit me right in the chest and I wince. "You turned me against myself. And for that, it is hard for me to forgive you. But I am willing to give you another chance. But I want proof of your love. I want you to show me that what you say is true, that you can't live without me, that you love me. And this time, I don't want it to be a secret. I don't want us to be a dirty secret."

***

CHAPTER TWENTY-NINE

MADELINE SCOTT

I came back home from the party feeling

better than I did before I went there. I didn't even

have much to drink, but I feel good. I feel amazing,

actually. I feel like myself after a very long time.

I didn't expect Steven to be jealous of Logan

and fight for me. I didn't expect him to confess his

love for me once again. And I sure as hell didn't

expect him to tell Gia to "fuck off" later. It was an

amazing experience. Overall, I loved it.

Gia's face when Steven announced me as his and his only was priceless. But his announcement is only the beginning of him trying to prove to me that he truly loves me, unlike the last time.

Emma and I came back home together with Lenny, so we got to dissect and talk about everything that happened at the party. Lenny was quite disappointed that he never knew that Steven and I had been dating. It was little comfort to him that nobody knew about our relationship other than Emma and Steven's three friends who had assumed from the way we behaved whenever we were together.

Logan had caught up with me after the whole announcement, letting me know that the only reason he agreed to dance with me was because he knew his friend needed an extra little push. I waved him off because I was embarrassed by the way my body reacted to him. But I know for a fact that my heart would have never belonged to him the way it did to Steven.

I changed out of my clothes, got into comfortable clothing, and slipped under the covers of my bed. I cuddled up to my pillows and closed my eyes, willing for sleep to come to me. But every time I closed my eyes, I saw Steven's pleading face float in my mind's eye.

I hadn't expected him to get down on his knees to beg to me. I hadn't expected him to say half the things that he said. Once upon a time, I would have taken his word for everything he said, but I can't bring myself to do that this time. This time, I need to know that what he says is the truth, and that he isn't playing games with me. I need to know that his love for me is true and he isn't going to make me a secret, hidden from the rest of the world.

I don't deserve that.

***

The class is so boring; I find myself wanting to nod off. I haven't been this bored ever before, and I have a feeling that it is because of how close finals are. These are some of the last classes in my last year, and I am sad as well as excited.

I am eager to get out into the real world, but I am also scared because things are about to get real. The world outside is not as forgiving as colleges and schools, and I am aware of it. To add to that, I want to start my acting career as soon as I get out of college, and I know it is going to be a pain in the ass to achieve my dream.

But I am willing to work for it. I am willing to be that person who strives until nothing is left of them. I want to be the one who gets to the top, even after getting messed up along the way.

The shrill ringing of the clock on the wall as it strikes three in the afternoon has the students packing up. The professor wishes us good luck with our exams before we scatter out of the classroom, eager to get to our residences to relax a little before diving back into our studies once again.

I walk out of the class to find Steven leaning against the door, a smile playing on his lips. He straightens when he sees me, stepping closer to me. The students around us pause to look at us before walking away, murmuring amongst themselves, but Steven doesn't seem to care.

"Your coffee, ma'am," he says, offering me the cup of coffee in his hand. It has been two weeks since the night of the party, and Steven has been bringing me coffee every single day without fail. And he no longer hides in empty classrooms and alcoves waiting for me to arrive, but waits for me until the end of the day, to hand me my coffee.

The last time, he made me feel like a thief whenever I took my coffee from him, but now, he is a changed man. He was serious when he said that he was willing to show me how I deserved to be treated.

"Thank you." I take the cup from his hand and begin to walk down the hall. He falls into step at my side, his hands behind his back.

"You're welcome. I was wondering if you want to watch a movie with me this evening," he says, glancing at me from the corner of his eyes. I look at him questioningly, and he rubs the back of his neck like he does when he is nervous. I suppress a chuckle as I pretend to think about it.

"Will you get me snacks?" I ask, and he grins, nodding his head.

"Of course, I will. Anything you want," he adds eagerly, and I let a small smile slip this time.

"Alright then. I will see you this evening." I pat him on the shoulder as I walk away from him. I am so happy that Steven is trying, truly trying to make it work with me this time. I was really sad at the prospect of losing him, but he had managed to bring back a little bit of hope into my life.

"Bye, Mads," I hear him call. Glancing over my shoulder, I wave to him before walking out of the building. Honestly, it is interesting to have a guy so obsessed with me.

***

I watch the same movie that I have seen many times before, but I don't complain as I sit by

Steven's side on his couch, with an assortment of snacks laid in front of us. The movie plays on the television in front of us, and I pretend to be interested when I am not. I would rather be doing anything but watching a movie right now.

Steven keeps stealing glances at me, and I don't want to let him down, so I continue watching the movie. I know I should probably tell him that I have watched it so many times that I remember the lines, but I don't open my mouth. Instead I keep reaching for the snacks and stuffing my face with them.

"How's your prep for finals going?" he asks me, and I am glad to have an excuse to look away from the screen.

"Good. It has been killing me though. What about you?" I ask him, tilting my head to the side. Steven shrugs, looking away from me.

"I am hanging in there," he answers. "I just started recently because I was in no shape to study after you left."

His admission makes my heart ache for him. I feel bad for walking away from him so promptly, so harshly, but I don't think we would be here, talking to each other, giving each other a second chance if I hadn't left him. Sometimes, people need to lose things that they love dearly to realize their importance. I needed to realize it, and so did Steven.

"I hope you are doing better now," I say, putting my hand on his. His gaze drops to my hand covering his, and he nods. His expression softens, opening up, and I find myself smiling too.

I am in love with this man. I realize this for the millionth time in the past few months. I am so in love with him that the thought of pushing him away is unbearable to me.

"I am doing a lot better now, mostly because I am trying to win you back. And you are letting me," he answers, and I can't help my cheeky grin.

"I knew you would be good at it." I pat him on the cheek. Steven scoots closer to me, a little bolder, and looks me in the eye, holding my hand to his cheek.

"How can I not be good at it? I have to get back the woman I love. I have to prove to you that this time, I am not willing to let you go, that I am not capable of it," he says, and my heart feels like it will explode in my chest any moment now.

I am extremely flattered by his confession. I want to kiss him, but that would be too much, right? I don't know. I just know that I want to be with Steven as much as he wants to be with me. In the two weeks I gave him, he has convinced me that he loves me still. He has proved his love to me.

"Steve?" I call his name as he continues to stare into my eyes.

"Hmm?" He responds, and I realize how much I have missed the sound. So beautiful, so deep.

I don't know how I thought I would be able to be with another man who wasn't him. I don't know how I convinced myself to leave him behind. I don't know how I was willing to give another man a chance knowing that I will always, always look at Steven.

"Do you love me?" I ask him. It is a stupid question because he has already proved to me that he does, but I just need him to say it again.

"More than I have ever loved anything," he replies, making a blush creep up to my cheeks.

"Do you want me?" I ask next. He continues to hold my hand against his cheek as he nods.

"More than I have ever wanted anything," he repeats.

I feel myself inching closer to him as if my body has a mind of its own. I just know that I need to feel him, that I need him by my side, his skin on my skin, and his lips on my lips.

I want to be one with him and never be away from him again.

"Steve, you have brought out the worst in me. But it is for my own good because I don't think I would have ever tried to be so resilient, so strong if it weren't for you," I say slowly, and Steven's eyes widen a little.

"I know I said that you made me hate myself and it's true, but I don't think I would have been able to realize my worth, my strengths if I hadn't been weakened. I forgive you for trying to protect me and yourself from the world, but I do want to stay by your side and take the world on together now." I offer him a small smile that seems to light up his mood.

"I want to face the best and the worst together for the sake of the friendship we have built, the feelings we have for each other, and the love we hold in our hearts for each other. Steven Jones, I am in love with you, you bastard, and it's all your fault." I laugh as I lean forward and capture his lips in mine.

Steven mumbles his "I love you" against my lips as he pulls me closer to him, the movie forgotten. I didn't plan for this to happen when I came to his house for a movie night, but I didn't expect to fall for him three years ago either. I didn't expect to date him either. And I didn't expect to love him either. But here we are. And I am not complaining. At all.

***

EPILOGUE

Steven Jones

I rub my eyes, squinting at the sun's rays that fall onto the bed, waking me up from sweet, sweet sleep. The coziness of the comforter and the perfect temperature of the room make me want to be buried under the covers all day long, but I have practice, and I need to get to the field before Coach calls me and decides to give me a lecture.

But I can spare a few more minutes.

I turn to my side and wrap my arm around my girlfriend's waist, pulling her into me. Maddy groans a little, protesting, but then she melts in my embrace as she turns to face me.

"You woke me up," she complains. I lean forward and place a kiss on her lips, not caring about morning breath.

It has been four years since we've been dating, so morning breath is the least of my concerns now.

"You need to get to the set, baby," I remind her gently, pushing her red hair out of her face. Her eyes fly open then, widening slightly as she realizes what day it is.

My little, beautiful, stunning, talented girlfriend is going to shoot her first movie today. Maddy's face lights up with a grin as she wraps her arms around me and hugs me.

"I am so excited! I can't believe I almost forgot about it," she squeals into my ear, and it is my favorite sound in the entire world. Other than her laugh, of course. Or when she sings in the shower. Alright, I can't choose. I love everything about her.

"It's okay. You spent last night fretting over it, before finally falling asleep well after midnight. I think you deserve to forget about it a little," I respond as she pulls away from me.

"And you have practice, mister. You have the league match this weekend. I don't want my boyfriend to lose, so get your ass up," she says as she gets out of bed. I groan, turning away from her.

But I want to stay in bed a little longer. After years of being disciplined and on time for practice every day, one would think I have gotten used to it. I haven't. I just manage to drag myself out of bed every morning. I am not a morning person.

Never was and never will be it seems.

After university, Maddy and I made our way through life together. We continued living in my house until I had to move out of California to play at the major leagues. Maddy followed me, chasing her acting career while supporting me.

We were separated for two years, doing long distance before she came back to live with me. She signed her first film two months ago after acting in commercials and side characters in various dramas and movies. This is her big break, and I am so excited for her.

Life has been good for Maddy and me. People who called us an odd couple and made fun of us now refer to us as the hottest celebrity couple. I am glad that we have moved past the difficult times in our lives and confident that we are strong enough to face difficulty if we are confronted by it.

I get out of bed and drag myself into the bathroom to get ready. Maddy is standing in front of the mirror, doing her skincare routine. I stare at her, leaning against the counter as I watch her because I love to see her take care of herself.

She hasn't changed. She is still as bubbly, beautiful, and authentic as she was before. She is real with her fans and now has them excited about the new movie in the making.

Maddy is still my Mads, and that is probably the most comforting thing in my life right now. I fell out with my parents after I told them that I was dating Maddy. They didn't approve of her and wanted me to find a better match for myself.

For the first time in my life, I stood up to them for my own happiness, and it felt good. Maddy didn't even know I told them about her until much later when I informed her that I won't be visiting my parents for the holidays anymore. But recently, they have reached out to me and apologized.

I have a feeling their sudden change of heart is the result of my girlfriend being all over the news for her amazing achievements, but I don't really care. I missed my parents despite everything they did to me, and I am glad they are coming around. They don't have the hold on me like they did before, and that is all that matters to me.

"What are you staring at?" Maddy asks when I keep looking at her with a smile on my lips.

"I can't believe you are mine," I answer, and a flush creeps up her neck. She lowers her head slightly, blushing, and I feel a burst of affection toward her.

I take a step closer to her, wrapping my arms around her as I look at her reflection in the mirror.

"I am so in love with you, Maddy," I add. She tilts her head and places a kiss on my cheek, patting my other cheek with her hand. It is a loving gesture of hers that I absolutely adore, and she knows how much I love it, so she does it again.

"Good. Because I am in love with you too," she replies, and I grin, letting myself feel grateful for everything I have. Especially her.

***

Madeline Scott

I massage my neck subtly as I walk onto the rooftop of the restaurant where I am supposed to meet Steven and our friends. I was supposed to arrive with my boyfriend, but I got caught up on the set. I never thought life as an actor would be so hectic.

I am exhausted, though, and would love to go

home and get into bed with my love, instead of having dinner with our friends. I love our friends, don't get me wrong, but right now, I am just really, really tired. The day dragged on today, and I didn't get to rest, for even a minute.

As I walk across the floor of the beautiful restaurant, I immediately find my friends. They are all gathered around a small podium, and I frown, wondering why on earth they are not seated already.

I spot Emma first, and she grins, making her way over to me and engulfing me in a huge hug. I melt into her embrace as I feel the years of friendship, happiness, and fun rush back to meet me. It is no surprise that Emma and I stayed friends even after college came to an end.

She is now a renowned painter in NYC who has her own gallery and does shows and teaches a select group of prodigies, every now and then. She has succeeded in life, and I am so happy for her. Beside Emma stands Jared and Gianna, the couple from our university. They are married now, and Gianna is pregnant with their first child.

Jared is a successful businessman, and Gianna is a fashion designer. I love how all of our friends got to where they wanted to be in life even though the odds were stacked against them in so many ways, mostly relating to Steven and me.

Logan is the last one in our small group. He is a soccer player like Steven, they were even on the same team. We meet from time to time, and he has grown to become my boyfriend's closest confidante, other than me, of course.

I greet each one of them with the same level of enthusiasm that I showed when we were in college together. Sometimes, I can't believe that we are all together in the end, happy and thriving in our lives.

"Where are your partners?" I ask Emma and Logan. I was expecting to see their partners too, and now I am disappointed because I have come to love Logan's girlfriend, Jacqueline. She is a total vibe, and I love discussing fashion and movies with her. She is Logan's assistant and his fiancée, and we all love her so much!

"Lenny couldn't make it, since he has a show tomorrow, and the guys need to practice," Emma replies, referring to her boyfriend's band, which is also doing pretty well.

"Jacqueline is at her parents' house this weekend. I let her be since Steven called me here in an emergency," Logan answers, although he doesn't sound too pleased to have to be away from his fiancée. I nod my head in understanding as I scan the crowd.

"Where is my boyfriend?" I ask, searching for a handsome face in the crowd of the man who owns my heart.

"Here I am," Steven's voice comes through a microphone, and I frown. I can't see him, but then the podium behind my friends begins to rise, and they part as if on cue to give way to my boyfriend.

Steven rises onto the podium wearing a tuxedo and kneeling on one knee on the ground. My heart skips several beats as I realize what is happening.

"This was all his plan," Logan murmurs in my ear, but I barely hear him, my eyes fixed on the man in front of me who is facing me now.

"Surprise!" Emma squeals softly in my other

ear, but I don't react to her either. All I can do is hold my breath and stare at Steven.

"Maddy, you and I have been together for four years. And when we first got together, I hid you away from the world, even though you meant the world to me," my boyfriend says, and my heart kicks into overdrive. "You left me because I was ashamed of being with you in front of others, because I was ashamed of myself. Four years have gone by, baby, after you gave me a second chance."

"Every day I wake up next to you, I am grateful to you for giving me that second chance because if it weren't for it, I wouldn't be here tonight, asking you the question that will make or break me. So tonight, I ask you in front of the world, Mads. Will you marry me?" he asks, and silence falls over the rooftop.

Even the music pauses, and people wait for

my response. I swallow as a thousand emotions swarm me at once. I am aware of the cameras on us and am aware that we are going to be in the headlines tomorrow. Steven really just announced our love to the whole world, permanently.

My chin wobbles, and I feel my answer bubbling in my chest. Steven's hopeful face is crowded with worry when I don't speak right away, but when I do, I say it with every fiber of my being, sealing our fate.

"Yes, I will marry you." And then celebrations erupt around us. My boyfriend—now my fiancé— places the ring on my finger, and I let the tears fall then, grinning from ear to ear.

Our friends congratulate us, teasing me because apparently, everyone knew that Steven was going to propose tonight, except for me. I cry tears of joy as I hug Steven once before capturing his lips with mine. He granted me my wish for so long, respected it, and let me have my happiness. The whole world knows today. Madeline Scott was made for Steven Jones. And Steven Jones loves Madeline Scott.

*** THE END***

ABOUT THE AUTHOR

Kathy Winslower is a gifted storyteller with a passion for weaving tales of love, resilience, and triumph. With her captivating narratives and richly drawn characters, she takes readers on unforgettable journeys that explore the depths of human emotions and the power of love to transform lives.

Born with an insatiable curiosity and a love for words, Kathy began her writing journey at a young age, filling countless notebooks with her imaginative stories. As she grew older, her passion for storytelling only deepened, leading her to pursue a career as a novelist.

Drawing inspiration from her own experiences and the world around her, Kathy's writing is characterized by its heartfelt authenticity and emotional depth. She skillfully delves into the complexities of relationships, capturing the raw and tender moments that shape her characters' lives.

When she's not immersed in her writing, Kathy can be found exploring nature, seeking inspiration from the beauty of the world around her. She believes that every moment holds the potential for a story, and it is her mission to capture those moments and share them with her readers.

www.ingramcontent.com/pod-product-compliance
Lightning Source LLC
Chambersburg PA
CBHW072038190726
48294CB00005B/1307